Devoluti...

Written History Is Unfounded

By

RN Vooght

Editor: A Kusevra

Contact: utteredit@gmail.com

Copyright © 2015 RN Vooght

All rights reserved.

ISBN: 978-1983809361

Prologue

The Blue Planet, a giant menacing sphere of fire and destruction hurtling silently through the infinite void of time and space.

Clouds of fury ravaged the globe for centuries, and scorched the ancient lands of a bitter past. Violent earthquakes twisted the beauty of what had been, as the oceans swallowed cultured civilisations whole.

In time, this violent constant would eventually succumb to the natural cycle of the planets processional clock, thus restoring a utopian sense of harmony once again within the natural world.

No one knew what *really* happened. Although everyone knew it would. Many of those who remained eventually fell foul to famine and disease; but we're a stubborn breed, humankind. Those who lived out their lives away from the civilised world on higher plateaus and shunned modern society had survived. They sought refuge in cave dwellings and returned to their hunter-gatherer roots, the written word forgotten. Only survival mattered now. Far less than one percent of the global population had survived the cataclysm - but, survive they did.

The end of days was a long time ago now.

Millennia have since passed.

1

Toli shuddered as he craned his neck, trying to keep his focus on the small bundle of assembled kindling and fire wood he'd placed beneath the reassuring glow of the moon. There was a familiar chill in the dusky gloom of the rainforest and a cool breeze licked at Toli's bare legs as he pondered the breaking dawn. Instead of the deafening chorus of the thousands of unseen night creatures in search of a mate, the lush canopy had fallen eerily silent, except the muffled cries of howler monkeys in the distance. Screwing up one side of his dusty adolescent face, Toli leaned into the breeze and listened. Drums. It was a cold and unfamiliar rhythm, distant but certainly there. He winced as he grated his bare skin on the harsh ground beneath him and brushed his knees free of the accumulated crushed rainforest that stabbed at his skin. He peered into the misty twilight adjusting his gaze. A distant rolling thunder, maybe? No. Drums. The need for warmth now only a distant memory and his pulse quickened as he sprang to his feet quickly stretching away the memory of an uncomfortable night. Clearing his nose free of an itch, Toli swept the greasy matted hair from his face and lurched nimbly into the night. Familiar voices were stirring in the blackness around him and he jumped at his own hazy reflection leaping across a cold shallow stream that wound its way slowly but surely to the sea. One day, Toli had promised himself, his heart would follow that stream. Ignoring a stitch in his side, he darted into a shadowed clearing, avoiding the low hanging branches that pointed their way towards Toli's destination.

Drums. Toli stood at the foot of the ancient stone megalith his people had adopted centuries before. Ritual sacrifices were held at the summit, celebrating the equinoxes and the promise of rain. A blood-letting of hundreds of virginal souls, offering their still beating hearts as gifts to appease the Gods whom built it - in a time forgot. The Gods were truly powerful.

Strange, yet beautifully crafted, short interlinked patterns adorned the structures ageing limestone surface, which boldly stepped skywards on four sides piercing the jungle canopy and reached for the stars.

Toli spat on the tips of his fingers and thrust himself up the first few giant steps, his people looking curiously ant-like in the gloom below him as he climbed.

Drums. The rhythmic pounding becoming louder, more menacing, frightening even. Never in Toli's short life had he heard such a dreadful sound. He thought his heart would burst in his chest as he scrambled atop the looming edifice, kicking loose stones into the darkness below.

At the summit a sea of torch light could be seen beneath the broken canopy of what he considered to be his home. Slowly advancing. The drums growing ever louder like a distant thunder, slowly rolling towards him.

Could this be what his people had been waiting for, praying for even? Stories of the Gods one day returning were known to everyone. Bearded pale-faced ancestors of a land unknown had taught Toli's fore fathers to shape the land, and craft its natural waterways into manageable canals. They had learned the importance of cultivation and irrigation, a means with which to hunt, and animal husbandry. The very foundation of this utopian like civilisation, were seeded by the very hands of the Gods. Story tellers told of their return from across the oceans, to once again be heralded the savior of them all. What troubled Toli though were the other stories. His mind was racing and he was no longer cold. But he was certainly shaking.

The Gods? Had they returned?

2

Choku understood the importance of ritual. Never, in his sixty something years had he dared dream that he would one day, be bestowed the honor of welcoming the return of the Gods. Dressed in bright plumed feathers and razor like teeth from a jaguars jaw, his body writhed and jerked as his toothless gums spat incantations from the depths of his soul. The pale faces marched unblinkingly behind him as he leapt and danced and rattled undecipherable echoes into the eerie twilight. Choku was swelling with pride as he unknowingly led this party of stone faced assassins into the heart of his people's homeland.

Dawn had broken for the last time, but nobody knew it. Toli stood in open mouthed silence wondering if all Gods adorned such a shimmering, unnatural looking torso and headdress. Banners snapped in the wind as five hundred pale faces drank in the wonders of this strange new paradise, standing in perfectly formed ranks despite the overwhelming number of fearsome painted faces that encompassed them. Unbeknownst to the welcoming faces of the bronzed natives, the strange looking visitors were here for a very different reason. Gold. And it stretched almost as far as the eye could see. They had certainly won it all, and it would be like taking candy from a child. These simple open armed fools had no idea of their fate, yet they sang and chanted in a guttural tongue that confounded the most intelligent of these hardened warriors.

3

Ocha had never enjoyed his so called birth right. Since the unforeseen death of his father several years before, he had accepted the responsibility half-heartedly at best. He cut a lean figure in his prime but years of unbroken sun had baked his skin dark and hard, and his boney frame sank into the ornate features of his jade throne. Ocha sat nervously eyeing his people ceremoniously placing delicate offerings at the feet of the returning Gods. Children jostled for position to catch a glimpse of the tribes certain savior. They would no longer be hungry as the Gods would surely bring the rains with them.

Something didn't sit quite right with Toli, as he eyed the long, strange looking decoration hanging from each of these Gods' hip plates, and he cautiously descended his lofty perch. At the foot of the pyramid Choku skipped by him in a trance like stupor, still crying out to the heavens above, his eyes taking on a haunting possession. Every one of these Gods to a man had his right hand resting on the hilt of his shimmering decoration and a hollow chill swept through Toli, as his gaze met with one his saviors. Still they sang, and some of the women shared tears of joy as Toli slipped out of the suffocating space and Choku collapsed at the foot of Ocha's throne.

Silence. A broad framed bull of a man stepped forward from the assembled Gods and Toli skirted the gathering crowd to the threshold of the still dark jungle. The silence was deafening. Ocha flexed his stiffening back muscles, inhaled sharply through the elaborate piercing in his nose and stood, casting a muted look of wonderment over the gathered ensemble. Splendidly coloured feathers of blue, yellow and green swayed lazily next to the braided tail of thick black hair which snaked down Ocha's spine. His palms open and facing the sky arms wide, Ocha closed his eyes and slowly knelt on the rough surface beneath his bare feet.

Now only the gods remained standing as Ocha's people followed suit and bowed deeply, each man, woman and child placing their foreheads on the cold hard earth. Toli clutched a loose hanging vine frozen in terror as the burly looking God unsheathed his decorative spear head, longer than a man's arm and raised it above his armored head piece. Ocha never even knew it happened. The blade came down silent and true, sending Ocha's soul to the spirit world in half a beat of his trusting heart. Toli was paralyzed in fright as his bladder failed him and he slumped to his knees. Kochu rose in a bewildered rage, his eyes ravaged with blood lust and fear. The iron hilt of the deceitful Gods blood red sword cracked his skull with a hollow thud that hammered Kochu into the afterlife. Like giant metallic wasps, the ranks broke as one. Five hundred shimmering warriors hacked their way into the confused, panic stricken, crowd that had assembled to witness the return of the Gods.

Confusion reigned amongst the muted cries of Toli's people, as the glittering warriors from afar cut and slashed with a ruthless efficiency. The men of the tribe fought in vain. Arrows and hunting spear alike glanced harmlessly from cold metallic torsos, piercing only the cool morning air as their targets effortlessly quenched their thirst for blood and destruction. Toli was snapped from his reverie as he heard the twisted cry of the voice that had raised him. His mother stood glassy eyed, slowly sinking to her knees, his world crashing in around him. Toli skidded from the brush, kicking up the dust amongst the press of grief stricken tribesmen being swatted from their idyllic worlds. A burning desire to reach his mother consumed him as the tip of a silent blade licked the side of his leg. He wiped the stinging sweat from his brow with the realisation of what he did not wish to be true. Toli's mother smiled with recognition, her eyes fading and finding an odd kind of peace from within her. She slumped forward revealing the gash that had opened her from neck to hip, now lying motionless on the blood red earth. A mindless uncontrollable desire to be away from this maddening place gripped Toli, and he dashed afoot the sun drenched pyramid feeling the onset of weakness in this thigh. The Gods were ruthless. The pale face appeared from nowhere before him, slashing his murderous side arm powerfully downwards. Toli's strength in his legs failed him as he slipped on a dark sticky pool of blood, where an elder's throat had been spilled on the causeway beneath him and he crashed to the ground fearing the end. Cold steel on granite. Toli peered terrified through clenched eyes, wondering how he was still alive. The warrior's sword had cut free a slim conical looking piece of granite which had protruded from the base of the pyramid. It had certainly saved him and Toli swiped it up and swung it in a wide arc burying the top half beneath an exposed piece of flesh between the warrior's protective plates of armor. The warrior reeled in pain as Toli pulled it free and struggled to his feet. He ducked another blow still clutching his ornate looking weapon, and brushed aside the razor-like creeping vines like a curtain and splashed into the stream as he struggled to breathe. Then there was darkness. There was no pain as Toli crashed into the icy water, a spear piercing him between his shoulders. He would find peace now and maybe his mother again, as his slowing heart bled crimson and followed the ceaseless flow of the stream, and his dreams. His lifeless eyes stared vacantly at the curiously inscribed piece of granite which rested inches from his face. Toli would watch over it for the next five hundred years.

A dull murmur of thunder rumbled in the dirty looking clouds above one of the city's many universities. It had rained for what felt like a lifetime and Hannah rolled her eyes and gazed upwards. The sky had always seemed to be crying.

"Just another day in paradise," she uttered to herself placing a newspaper above her shaved head and smiling at the irony. She felt it would have been two years wasted, had she not thrown up over the ever popular Alex, now her boyfriend, at an unauthorised campus party almost a year to the day. He was the one, she was certain of it. They'd studied computer programming and mathematics together, and yet prior to this morning's untimely dismissal for an appalling attendance record, Hannah couldn't help wonder if Alex would fall victim to the same fate.

Alex had cut class for the fourth time in as many days, only sending vague responses to the many text and voice messages Hannah had left over the same period. It was Hannah's birthday the coming weekend and her mind ran wild with expectation as to what Alex could possibly be planning. Lightening cracked somewhere above, and Hannah reigned in the collar of her old navy Cargo jacket as she splashed down the university steps two at time, cutting a path a few blocks across town to Alex's apartment. It was rush hour at every hour in the city that never sleeps, and the lightening cut photographic stills of rain sodden faces making their way home beneath the cold grey skyline.

"The end is nigh…!" a homeless soul wailed, thrusting a small damp flyer into Hannah's hand. Musty, week old sweat stabbed at Hannah's senses as he grabbed at her fraying coat sleeve. "For most of us…!" the yellow, tobacco-stained, teeth hissed at her. She twisted free of his grip, stuffing the piece of paper into her pocket and spinning away as her dated cell phone rattled into life.

"Heya Spam, how's it going? Are you still coming tonight?" quizzed a familiar voice on the other end of the line. Hannah hated the nickname, but 'Spam' had stuck like unwanted spilled glue from a private joke between the two life-long friends, although Sammy had always used it affectionately, regardless.

"Oh shit, sorry hun, I forgot all about this evening!" Hannah replied, "I've not seen or heard from Alex for the best part of the week so I'm heading over there now. I think he's planning something big for my birthday or at least, I hope he is. I'll make it up to you Sammy, I promise!"

There was a long pause, "Sam, you still there?" Hannah prompted.

"You were meant to be making it up to me *this* time Spam, never mind. Hope dream boy is worth it! Love you loads, call me." There was a click and the phone was dead. Sammy was Hannah's dearest friend and was always a million miles an hour, a dedicated activist trying to change the world, always fighting for this or rallying for that. It was true Hannah had let her down more times than she could remember, but she'd make things right one day, she was certain. It just seemed that Alex was the more important cause at this particular time in her life.

5

Wet through, Hannah pushed her spare key into the lock, turned the barrel and silently crept across the threshold.

The lights were dimmed and two glasses sat on the table next to an empty wine bottle and discarded take away food cartons. The scent of a smouldering candle filled the air along with the sound of contented giggling as rain lashed against the window outside. A muffled rumble of thunder made Hannah shiver as blinking lightening lit up the clothes strewn hallway to Alex's bedroom.

"Bastard!" she stifled through gritted teeth placing the key into one of the wine glasses, tears slowly breaking onto her already wet cheeks.

Feeling both hollow and numb, Hannah found herself standing, almost swaying at the foot of the old apartment block. Her day old make-up creating black tears as she fumbled for her phone once again, trying not to pay attention to her shaking hands. "S-Sam, Sam, he..." Hannah choked off before she could summon the right words.

"Aw, baby bird. They're all the same, he didn't deserve you anyway I bet he..."

Hannah broke in, "I've had enough Sam, that's it. I honestly believed..." She wiped her eyes and snivelled into the handset, "It feels like the end of the world!"

"You might not want to joke about that sort of thing Spam, you don't realise how close we possibly are!" Sammy asserted.

"Possibly are what?" Hannah scoffed.

"Where are you? Can you get to City Hall as soon as you can? I think there's a... " Sammy's voice cut off mid-sentence, the line hissed and crackled, then went dead.

"Sammy? Sam? Oh, wonderful!" muttered Hannah sarcastically, shaking the phone as if it would make a difference to the connection. "Taxi!" she shouted in vain as a grubby cab sped past, kicking up an oily slick in its wake. A burst of car horn startled Hannah and she span on the spot, suddenly realising she was standing in the middle of the street. The driver sat clutching the wheel shaking his head in time with the hypnotic windshield wipers. Stepping aside apologetically, she trotted briskly towards a taxi cab across the street. The light atop the taxi was switched off but it couldn't hurt to ask Hannah thought, wiping her eyes free of the black stains with her now heavy rain sodden cargo sleeve. "I need to get to City Hall, rather quickly!" she stammered, climbing into the musty smoke filled interior.

"I'm clocked off lady, sorry. You'll probably get there quicker on the subway anyhow at this time of night," the cab driver asserted, flicking a half-smoked cigarette clear out of his window. "Why City Hall, if you don't mind me asking? I mean, it's Friday night after all."

"I'm not sure myself yet," Hannah perplexed, looking at her cell phone with frustration.

The dashboard radio went on, unnoticed; "With strained resources and global pollution rife, world energy magnates are set for crisis talks amid the escalating fears of global nuclear warfare. Worldwide crop failures and depleted oil reserves have put the nation on high alert for possible…"

"I live two blocks up from City Hall, honey…" the driver said, turning down the radio, "You look like you've had it rough today, this ones on me!" The taxi screeched into life, made a U-turn and was swallowed in the throng of bustling city traffic, as Hannah stared, vacantly, through a side window heavy with condensation.

6

City Hall loomed grey and unwelcoming, occasionally bursting to life in the crashing thunder and lightning. Its giant marble pillars stood in silent authority, slick with rain as an organised party of demonstrators thrust carefully worded banners of protest and vexed voices towards the gathered paparazzi and assembled police line. Inside, the master of ceremonies stood before a packed auditorium and introduced the first of the evening's guest speakers. "And without further ado, please welcome to the stage esteemed geologist and physicist Professor L C Halliday." The assembled audience rose to their feet in a wave of applause as the Professor paced nervously back stage, fumbling with a fist full of notes for the evening's lecture and pointlessly re-adjusting his wire-rimmed glasses. In his mid-thirties, Professor Halliday had been a rising star in his chosen fields of study until he was publicly ridiculed on his theories of an impending global cataclysm and that we were the true architects of our own imminent demise. His argument had started gathering pace out of the public eye with both academics and conspiracy theorists alike. But since his work had been published eighteen months before, Professor Halliday had found himself the target of unseen powerful political figures of authority. He unconsciously scratched at his greying goatee and loosened the neck tie that seemed to be suffocating him. He wasn't comfortable in the borrowed dinner jacket and longed to be back in the rain forests of the southern hemisphere in his khaki's and twenty something year old wrangler hat. Public engagements terrified him. "Sammy, where are you?" he fretted quietly, between clenched teeth, trying to bite at the thumbnail that had been gradually gnawed away as he waited to take to the stage. Thirteen years his junior, he had met Sammy by chance on a field trip half the world away. She was campaigning with the now underground movement Earth Party, in protest against the assembly of nuclear reactors in one of the planets last remaining natural wildernesses.

He had been overseeing the excavation of an ancient and still undated stone construction, which was in the path of the newly planned reactor site when their worlds collided. He had looked upon her with the eyes of a protective older brother at first, hiding his feelings because of the difference in years between them. But after months of Sammy's jovial banter and undiscouraged advances, the Professor had thrown caution to the wind, and tumbled head first into a romance that had given him the confidence to enter the public domain once again. Although he knew she couldn't resist being in the thick of the protestations which had engulfed City Hall, she had assured him that she would take her place front of house in the auditorium to distract him from the thousands of baying eyes that had gathered for the evening's event.

Deafening applause snapped Halliday into the present with a start as he was introduced. He took a deep breath, running his fingers through his thick mop of hair and squinted as he stalked towards the podium amid blinding lights and camera flashes.

7

Outside, Sammy was caught in the crushing press of protesters, lost in a sea of banners proclaiming a revolution as their solution. Hundreds, perhaps thousands of angry faces vented their frustration with strained voices in front of the assembled media in support of the non-televised event taking place within. The demonstration had originally been planned to peacefully highlight to the ill-informed public, about the escalating fears of depleted world resources, and that the supposed elected members of society's governing elite were turning a blind eye for nothing more than profit. Sammy had organised and attended countless protests in the past and had found them both fulfilling and exhilarating. Yet she could not suppress the feeling that this particular rally was beginning to spiral out of control, and was terrified that it would be reported by the media's puppet masters as nothing more than a damning group of unwashed, mislead rebels without a cause. Tempers were beginning to fray as teams of tactically astute riot police were manoeuvring into well-rehearsed formations with water cannons despite the torrent of rain, as thunder boomed overhead. Sammy's attention was suddenly drawn to an unnervingly calm looking face moving through the crowd, paying almost no mind to what was happening around him. An athletic build and steely cold set jaw, the man scanned his surroundings, tilted his head to his collar and appeared to speak whilst straightening the heavy looking red duffel bag which was slung across his shoulder. A police bullhorn broke into life uttering inaudible threats above the mounting madness outside City Hall. Sammy was almost knocked from her feet by an over enthusiastic riot officer on horseback lurching into her side-on. Oddly it seemed to be the police that were the cause of the chaos and not the protestors, Sammy realised. A burst of paparazzi flash-light jolted her back to her original focal point, now lost from view. "Where the..?" Sammy began, as she pulled her vibrating cell phone from her cropped leather jacket pocket. She briskly unlocked the luminescent screen with her thumbprint I.D. and placed it to her ear. "Aw, baby bird! They're all the same, he didn't deserve you anyway I bet he….." said Sammy, still scanning the crowd for the red backpack. "You might not want to joke about that sort of thing Spam, you don't realise how close we possibly are!" she continued. "Where are you? Can you get to City Hall as soon as you can? I think there's a…" this time Sammy was crashed to the ground in the press of protestors as the police whipped up an almost violent frenzy around her. Pinned by an unseen force, Sammy's cheek was burned by a rough friction as a red shoulder strap was grated against her face. As she attempted to free herself from the jostling crowds encumberance, she twisted onto her side and glimpsed a four fingered hand wrench the backpack free from beneath her, splitting its side and revealing its frightening contents. The bag was lost from view as the man stuffed the series of wires and flashing LED back inside, and melted back into the surmounting madness.

8

After a stuttered introduction L.C. Halliday had fumbled his way through to his fourth page of notes which Sammy had helped piece together with him the night before. She said she would be here. He surveyed his current page and looked out over the rim of his shabby glasses and continued. "I believe there is a shift in consciousness, regarding global awareness and resistance to the continuation of an economic system which values profit at the expense of the people and all life on this planet." The auditorium was his. He ruffled his papers loosening a knot in his side, and cleared his throat. "Fully aware of the problems we face with over population on a planet with finite resources, we continue to burn de-pleating fossil fuel reserves and ever increasing deforestation has ripped the lungs out of the planet. We've almost completely poisoned our oceans, lakes and rivers. We are at war with the planet and most of you are blind to species extinction which is now occurring on a daily basis. Yet we sit proud of our achievements. The creation of atomic energy as an alternative to baron oil wells scattered about the Earth.

We are the masters of our own destiny. But there's a curve ball! I spoke of extinction, ladies and gentlemen." Halliday paused eyeing the front row. Sammy was nowhere to be seen. "We're next!" There was mixed emotion from the packed hall, murmurs of discontent and hecklers, even laughter as others only straightened their backs and sharpened their hearing. "We can either continue to turn a blind eye or unite on a global level and restore the planet to its former glory and prosper, as the ancients did in times untold! They were the true masters of their own prospering destiny, an undisclosed civilisation at a technological peak which worked with each other in harmony with the planet and not against one another. The truth has been buried from us and history is incorrect!" he soaked in the stunned faces of the packed auditorium. "But, I believe there is another way!" his audience was baited.

9

Sammy wriggled to her feet, prodding at the stinging graze on her cheek and cleared her head. "Holy shit!" she exclaimed only now realising the gravity of the situation. Where'd he go? She had to find him, this cold and calculated figure with a clear desire to kill and maim. This was meant to be a peaceful demo, they always were - it didn't make any sense. Gripping the back of a ruffled rain coat, Sammy hoisted herself above the heads of banner touting strangers and balanced on the rusty old fire hydrant beneath her feet. "Come on, come on, where the hell..?" she grimaced in frustration, scanning the rain lashed crowd. There! The man unwittingly marked himself out as he gestured towards his collar once again - eyes always darting behind mirrored lenses and heavy-set lids. He still had the red bag too, tucked under his right arm and concealing the frightful contents from view.

Sammy dismounted the fire hydrant and fumbled through the contact index of her cell phone, and put the receiver to her ear. "Come on, come on, pick up, pick up!" Sammy almost growled through gritted teeth, her heart pounding inside her chest. Without warning, another surge from the frenzied crowd knocked the handset from her grasp and it skittered out of view. "Shit!" she exclaimed, searching frantically in vain, still being pushed and bumped from side to side. There wasn't time enough to fret about the loss of her phone. Sammy took a deep breath and swore inwardly as she cautiously stalked through the baying crowd towards the large man.

10

Half a block away an old yellow taxi which had seen better days coasted up to a puddled sidewalk and lurched to a halt, the wipers still idly swishing their thankless task. "Okay, this is me lady. City Hall is only another..." yelled the driver, trying to keep his own cigarette smoke from going into his eyes.

"Yes I know," Hannah interrupted, "but are you sure about the fare? I mean, it's only *fair!*" Hannah cringed at her own joke and broke a wry smile.

"Get outta here, you," he coughed. "And try keeping that

smile. It's a tiny ray of sunshine in this God forsaken city, now go on, beat it!" Hannah widened her smile in reply as she stepped from the cab, leaving a crumpled note on the back seat, barely enough for a coffee but a small tip all the same. She tried in vain to reach Sammy on her cell phone but the line kept putting her straight to voice mail. "Hi, this is Sammy. Leave a message!": Beep!...

"Heya babe, it's Hannah," she started, "I'm almost there! Don't go changing the world without me!" She slid the phone into her inside jacket pocket cursing at the weather and broke into a trot as she headed towards the rear of the protesting ensemble. It looked like chaos, not the kind of 'Save the Planet' peace demonstration Sammy was always rallying on about. On another night Hannah would probably have thought better of trying to find her amongst the mob, but on this occasion Sammy would be missing the demo outside and sitting in starry eyed adulation while her apparent boyfriend wittered on, inside the building. Hannah pressed deeper into the buzzing crowd and pushed the sour thoughts of her own relationship to the back of her mind, as she wiped at her eyes, further smudging her makeup. She wrinkled her brow in confusion as she peered beneath her cupped hands and glimpsed the lime green leather jacket she'd leant Sammy the week before, precariously perched above the rest of the protesters, drop down disappearing into the mellay.

11

Within the auditorium Halliday pressed on, "This is old news, ladies and gentlemen. Very, old news indeed! It is my premise that we are not at the height of our own technological evolution as a species, absurd as this may sound. It is my premise that, the ancients - as we so fondly refer to them were far more technically advanced than we ever dared consider giving them recognition for. It is also my premise that the so-called 'powers that be' in today's circle of high society and manipulative powermongers, not only know about this ancient form of technology, a limitless and sustainable energy for the masses – but are doing everything within their power to keep this knowledge from us." He paused, "Why?" his eyes bore into the very souls of those assembled, and leaned accusingly on the podium for maximum effect. "Because, it is free…!"

An odd chill swept through the Professor as he fidgeted on the podium trying to respond to a swollen red-faced hog of a man, leaning forward in his seat and pushing his obese frame on his walking cane and sniggering. Halliday asserted, "Indeed sir, my work has been understandably ridiculed in the past but even as much as the people who accept the evolution theory's premise, without the infamous missing link that too is only mere speculation which has been interpreted as fact amongst the masses. Agreed, my theories concerning a lost civilisation as technologically advanced as our own if not more, would hold more water should I be able to produce the hard, irrefutable evidence that the ancients had thrived without draining the planet of its resources, yet were undone by a terrible natural disaster. Scholars far more qualified than myself have deciphered ancient texts depicting the end of times occurring over and over again. Whether it a deluge, the planet consumed in fire and destruction, a comet impact, the list goes on. These events have been essentially documented by our ancestors, sir. It is my belief that a certain re-cycling of life has taken place on the face this beautiful planet for millennia, because we just keep on destroying ourselves - all in the name of greed and profit. Ladies and gentlemen," he paused and swallowed hard, "it is

happening once again."

12

Sammy kept low and out of sight, partially hidden by the rain soaked banners that still bobbed up and down amongst the chaos. Her heart pounded in her chest as she manoeuvred through the crowd. Her head raced with a million different reasons to flee this horrifying situation, not understanding what she would do when confronted with this mysterious face of terror. Suddenly Sammy's world stopped. The blood in her veins turning to ice. Everything around her slowed as the nameless man turned towards her with a cold smile, the red bag gone. He pursed his lips to a fingerless hand and winked as he dissolved into the bodies around him. Sammy swallowed dryly as she saw the bag barely a few yards away, and heard only her own heartbeat.

13

Plexiglass riot shields now seemed to outnumber the boisterous crowd members as Hannah snaked out a path, desperately trying to close the gap on the green jacket. Hannah could barely hear herself think over the booming police loudhailer as she called out in vain. Lightning ripped through a dull burst of thunder and Hannah broke into a smile, realising the chase was finally over as Sammy stopped in her tracks barely twenty metres away and turned to face her. Sammy's face painted a picture of pure terror, and she was rooted to the spot. Emerging from the shadows an emotionless monster with mirrored eyes shoved Hannah aside with a powerful deformed hand and there was a blinding burst of light.

14

The same great sweaty oath kept picking at Halliday, shifting his weight whilst in his seat and fondling the offensively long pearl string attached to his monocle. It was this kind of uncomfortable stand-off which had spiralled out of control and almost shattered his reputation last time he went public with his research, and the hog-like gentleman was oddly familiar but unplaced in Halliday's mind. The Professor gripped at the podium stand and pleaded inwardly that Sammy were there to help counter argue this swine and his sniggering entourage. "Ironically," Halliday began, "it is often, no let me rephrase. Only, the wealthy and of privileged positions of power, such as my much esteemed gentleman may I presume, that find not fault with this theorem but presumably know there is another way because…" he broke off, with a shudder. Microphone feedback pierced every waiting ear and there were shrieks of horror and confusion as a wave of shock rippled through the amphitheatre. Uneasy audience members nervously stole a glance around and above. A giant glittering chandelier rocked heavily overhead and the Professor winced at recalling his own thoughts earlier that day whilst marvelling over such grand and ageing architecture. Again the microphone whistled and screeched, this time snapping Halliday back to the present. "What on....?" he asked, steadying himself and scanning the unfolding scene of disarray. Well-off hosts were hurriedly escorting their guests below dimly lit neon exit signs, and there were mutterings of a possible earthquake as lighting technicians sped past his peripheral vision hurrying to shut off the power to the staging area, in case of fire. Halliday stood clutching at the air, his papers erratically strewn across the stage floor. "Sssammy?" he stammered into life and bolted over the orchestra pit and up the steps towards the viewing gallery. She must still be outside. There was no secondary tremor, and having experienced many small quakes on expeditions in the jungles of the southern continent, he now feared a possible radical act of violence had taken place amongst the chaos outside. Emergency lighting flickered dully about him and Halliday picked his way through the pandemonium and out into the packed lobby of shouting and confusion. Light rain skirted the threshold of the large open doors to City Hall and the street, which only greeted him with a scene far worse than he dared imagine.

15

Beyond the heightening chaos and hysteria, a blacked out government plated automobile was illegally parked behind a prehistoric looking dumpster across the street. Agent Neville sat behind the leather steering wheel and cradled his cell phone on the stub of his pinkie. Droplets of rain hung from the tip of his nose and splashed on the display screen as he pondered the odd look of confusion on the face of the shaven headed young lady, before he had remotely detonated the bag. The call connected and Neville stiffened in his seat.

"Report!" Agent Neville heard from the now wet earpiece. He brushed it across his forearm drying it and returned it before speaking, "Package delivered. Carriage awaits." he affirmed.

There was a scoffed grunt of approval and then a click.

Agent Neville turned the ignition and flicked the wipers on to intermittent but kept the headlights off. He sighed tiresomely and slumped slightly in his seat, looking on as he awaited further instruction.

16

There was a muffled reverberating thud that seemed to be vibrating throughout Hannah's entire body. Had she passed out? She didn't feel dizzy. Her face stung and the stench of burnt flesh overwhelmed her senses and she reached a dry vomit, staggering to readdress her balance. Singed banners smouldered as wailing cries for help broke through the deafening ringing in her ears. The already assembled reporters excitedly pushed their camera lenses through the thinning smoke and gushed to the world, in over-speculated anticipation. Hannah went numb glimpsing a twisted lime green leather jacket lying prone on the sidewalk. A scattering of other bodies lay unnaturally crooked as tiny crisp red embers gently fluttered back to earth from above. Hannah gingerly made her way over to the jacket fighting her emotions and not wanting to look. Her bottom lip began to tremble and her eyes welled up as she stood over the familiar looking body hunched on its side. After composing herself with a few quick sharp breaths, she reached down and her heart jumped as Sammy spluttered a weak cough and tried rolling onto her back.

"Sam? Sammy? You're still…, Sam?" Hannah exclaimed almost in panic. "Can you hear me?"

"Spam!?!" Sammy choked, still on her side.

Hannah carefully levered Sammy over revealing a side of her face that she would not have recognised if not for the partially melted jacket. "Spam? Hannah, you're here?" Sammy tried.

"Yeah, it's me baby bird. It's okay." Hannah wrestled with tears. "You were just, you were just. I could see you. I don't know what happened Sammy, oh Sammy no!"

"I saw him Spam! I," Sammy coughed, "I saw him!"

"Saw who Sammy?" "You're gonna be okay!" Hannah gently ran her fingers through Sammy's matted hair fighting not to cry.

"He had a bag, Spam! It was in his duffel…" A paramedic siren gurgled into life somewhere in the middle distance and Sammy continued through the pain. "A red duffel, I saw it but the man with the hand he, he…Elsie was right, it was them Spam not us. The man with the hand, it's happened before!" Sammy fell unconscious, her pulse beating out a slowing rhythm in her neck as her head rolled to the side.

"Sammy hun? Stay with me, they're almost here. Sam? Sam?" Hannah looked up to see a local news crew poking their camera a little too close. "She needs help, not a front page you fuckin' idiots! Somebody *please* help!"

17

An all too keen young paparazzi maverick, chewing more gum than his mouth could hold came crashing out from the depths of his news van tripping on some surplus audio wiring as he hollered, "We got her! We got her!" his arms flailing.

His boss spoke whilst juggling a soggy cigar end between his teeth. "Her? What d'ya mean her kid?" He shuffled along the side of the van stepping over the same wires a little less awkwardly. "What you got?"

The technician was clearly shaking with excitement trying not to drop the monitor of stills taken moments before the explosion. Frozen in the centre of the screen was a picture of a tiny framed woman appearing to be almost hugging a red duffel bag with all too suspicious wiring exposed in the crush of protesters.

"Well I'll be damned! Great work kid! Peaceful demo my ass, we got the exclusive here. The Green Bomber! Ironic or what?" laughed the cigar toting paparazzi and stormed into the surrounding chaos, arms wild and dictating to his crew.

A familiar buzz was beginning to ripple through the media stations and word of the "Green Bomber" was out. Hannah reeled back in a rage as frenzied reporters started grappling at her accusingly whilst Sammy lay slumped at her feet. "She's one of them!" an enraged photographer announced, "There could be more!" Alarm bells pealed in Hannah's head as she digested the wayward accusations. Voices were becoming more strained and the atmosphere intensified. Now she was scared. She didn't yet understand what had happened but she was now afraid for her own life and fretted that Sammy could already be dead. "Over there!" Hannah screamed at the top of her lungs, pointing towards City Hall. She tore free of her captives and ducking beneath flailing arms Hannah sprung clear amid the chaos, her heart pounding with panic as she made off into the night.

18

The rain had eased a little and police lights shimmered in the puddles being stirred up amid the settling chaos. Professor Halliday stood swaying on the threshold of City Hall dwarfed by the slick marble pillars and trying to take in the devastation unfolding outside. He dialled and re-dialled Sammy's cell phone in the vain hope she would picked up if he tried just one more time. "Hi, this is Sammy…leave a message". Beep.

"Sammy," the Professor started, "it's me, call me I'm worried!" Returning the handset to his pocket he gingerly pressed into the throng of mounted riot police, and tried to suppress the knot of panic growing within him.

The Professor wandered the wreckage, suddenly seeing a young lady, wearing a rain lashed cargo jacket, frantically speed by and disappear from view. She appeared to be being pursued by a host of what looked like paparazzi. Halliday shook his head and pulled at a small handful of ringlets of hair in frustration and looked to the skies. Silently, he hoped Sammy was okay and that she'd maybe been arrested and would need bailing out later in the evening, as had happened in the not so distant past. He afforded himself a tight smile at the thought but was wrenched back to the present by the unmistakable burst of a paramedic horn which echoed beneath the flyover as it picked a slow path through the rain sodden ensemble. The night had started well but could now only possibly be spun into a media witch hunt that would once again end in Halliday falling on his own sword. The unreported story being that the corporate elite had once again succeeded in fooling the masses, by highlighting not the concept of a corrupt, profit driven government hell bent on destroying the planet once again, but of mindless terrorism at a rally of over qualified crackpots. His reputation would be in tatters, Sammy was missing and what he would do next was anybody's guess.

Disconcerted and somewhat dazed, Professor Halliday lowered himself and sat on the kerb, took off his spectacles and started to dry the lenses on the sleeve of his jacket, without much effect.

"Bravo Professor, cataclysmic indeed - wouldn't you agree?" there was a short intentional pause. "Now, get some rest Professor, I fear you may need it!" scoffed a jubilant voice, peppered with sarcasm. Halliday squinted upwards as a highly polished leather boot splashed down beside him and re-soaked his badly dried rims. An overweight hog of a man, somewhat familiar to him, continued to stride past while reseating his own diamond encrusted lens. He was eagerly followed by two stiff shouldered suits who kept cool trained eyes over the surroundings as they walked.

Halliday slowly rose to his feet and swept his hair from his face, and scratched at his forehead, grimacing. "Excuse me?" he shouted fiercely as he recoiled at the statement. "Who the hell are you?" he staggered forward hastily replacing his specs.

The Fat Man passed an old beaten up dumpster parked below the flyover. "The future!" he chuckled, disappearing as he ducked his head into the backseat of a blacked out car whose engine hummed quietly beside a familiar energy company motif, which buzzed in misfiring blue neon behind an electrical goods window. E.M. POWER. The Fat Man's stiff shouldered entourage followed suit and the vehicle silently wheeled into the distance.

Not far from a rusted old weather worn fire hydrant, the broken screen of a seemingly discarded cell phone blinked silently in the gloom. '2 New Messages.'

19

Hannah felt drunk on emotion. Her head was dizzy and

her eyes still stung a little, though she wasn't sure whether it was from her constant sobbing or the pungent stench of sulphur from the explosion that still lingered in her nostrils. As she huddled down by the canal she found her hands were shaking. She gulped down the clean air about her, trying desperately to calm her mind and her senses. She was sure she had lost the last of her pursuers a few blocks back, yet if she hadn't she very much doubted there was anything left in her tank to carry on running. Hannah told herself to calm down. Wiping her nose free of the accumulated snot and rain drops she rubbed at her wet leggings in a bid to keep warm. "What the hell just happened?" she thought to herself. How could a bad day get any worse? As if being kicked out of college wasn't bad enough! She'd caught her boyfriend cheating and just fled the scene of a possible terrorist attack on City Hall….labelled a possible suspect! And Sammy? God, was Sammy even still alive? She'd been a little incoherent but was muttering something about a 'red bag' and 'the man with the hand'. She felt she knew Sammy better than anyone else but had never heard of her speak of this *Elsie* before. "Elsie was right!" she'd said. But who was Elsie and what was she right about? The enormity of her situation was starting to hit her. Hannah half unzipped her jacket and reached in for her tobacco and promptly began to roll a cigarette, her hands still trembling. An old barge with more graffiti than original paintwork slowly slipped past and the rattle of steel tracks above her pounded out its crushing rhythm as carefree commuters made their way home on the subway system overhead. She felt tired but was abruptly jolted from her wandering mind as her head darted back towards the rear end of the passing barge to the sound of its nagging horn. More graffiti. Her subconscious alerted her though. 'The End?' was artistically sprawled across its bow. Hannah cocked her head to the side as she sat shivering and stared at the profound wording as it gurgled past, disappeared into the night. Lighting her damp cigarette it hit her. "The end is nigh...," the old vagrant had spluttered. Hannah inhaled sharply, pulling the rumpled flyer from her jacket, unravelling it. 'The End? Or A New Beginning?' read the headline atop the flyer. Emblazoned over what appeared to be an ancient step pyramid and unfamiliar symbolism were the words 'A lecture on the past to save the future, by Professor L.C. Halliday.' Hannah mustered a wry smile as she screwed up the piece of paper and stuffed it back in her pocket. "L.C.?" she whispered in a cloud of cigarette

smoke and closed her tired eyes.

20

Officer Harrison scanned the area on bended knee whilst stretching the cloudy talc soaked forensic gloves over his freckly fingers as he eyed the flashing handset, '2 New Messages.'

Harrison had only graduated from the academy the previous semester and felt wetter than his rain sodden, academy issued trench coat. It felt heavy on his hunched shoulders as he studied the discarded cell phone at his feet, yet the weight of expectancy at living up to his highly decorated father's service record felt like a burden he would never be able to shake free. An only child, Harrison had wanted for nothing, only for the ever present shadow of his father to disappear. The old man had been killed in the line of duty when he was three and it had always felt like he'd never even met the man. He pushed the suffocating thoughts of his father to the back of his mind, slipped the blinking cell into a wet evidence bag and rose to his feet surveying the area. "Why would a demonstrator detonate a devise amongst their own supporters?" he wondered, it made absolutely no sense. Should there have been a target they would certainly have been inside City Hall? Had the device detonated by mistake? It was puzzling to say the least. Speculating paparazzi were running away with their own theories, of course, and word of 'The Green Bomber' was on everyone's lips. Only one word was on Harrison's mind. Why?

He popped a stud on his sodden trench coat a slid the evidence bag inside. A weathered and gruff voice boomed at his side as a large hand clapped him on the back, knocking him off balance. "We'll be back at HQ for the end of the game now, Harry!" It was his Captain, Stacey. His face was lined like an old road map and droplets of rain hung in the silver beard which lined his twisted mouth. "We've already ascertained real time video footage of the suspect on scene – she'll be singing like a bird in custody by sunrise, an open and shut case kid!" Stacey cleared his thick steam filled glasses and continued. "Who's your money on? We gotta great defence this year, no?"

"She?" asked Harrison.

"The Green Bomber, they're calling her!" the captain fished for a cigarette in a damp box and lit it. "Fuckin' evangelists!" he stated drawing a long tired drag and ex-hailed as he spoke. "You reckon this rookie is gonna bring it home this year?"

"Bring it home? Capo, this Green…..?"

Stacey interrupted, "Hell yeah, you seen this guy's arm? It's like a God damned laser guided missile, shit I've never seen anything like it in my life…except maybe the old man! He could play ball for sure, until….!" He winced at bringing him up at such a delicate time and considered changing the subject, but the young officer beat him to it.

"Sir," Harrison broke in, "football's not really on my radar, I mean…"

Stacey boomed above his half-hearted response. "Just don't drop the ball like an asshole Harry!" "I didn't put you on this case, the call came from upstairs!" Stacey spat at Harrison's feet and pushed past.

"It's Harrison sir, not Harry!" Harrison said, barely audible.

"You're still an asshole!" The captain flicked the half smoked cigarette and a finger towards him, and disappeared into the blur of flickering blue lights.

A muffled vibration could be heard from somewhere around Harrisons midriff as patted at his trench coat. The cell phone was ringing.

21

A few blocks east, Professor Halliday sat in his overly tidy studio apartment staring vacantly at his long gone cold cup of filtered coffee. The last words Captain Stacey had expressed, rather accusingly, thought the Professor were "Don't go skipping town now Doc."

Halliday knew there would be questions and he certainly wanted the same answers, but what was going on? Was he been looked upon as a possible suspect? The thought of it seemed absurd, but this sort of thing had happened before and it nearly cost him his entire credibility. "I'm a Professor, not a bloody Doctorate!" he said, taking a cheap shot at the table beneath his hands, surprising himself at his own angry outburst. He frowned as he caught himself twisting his hair around his index finger in frustration, but Sammy wasn't there to tease him, though he wished she was. He kicked out his chair with the backs of his legs as he fumbled through his corduroy trousers and pulled his phone from a pocket of discarded gum wrappers and loose change. He stared at Sammy's name emblazoned the neon screen and hit redial. Tears welled in his eyes as he placed the cold plastic to his ear.

The call connected. Silence. The Professor hesitated

momentarily as it had almost caught him by surprise that it hadn't rung straight through to her answer phone. "Sammy?" Halliday almost whispered. Silence still. "Sammy, you okay?" he pushed.

"Professor?" an unmoved voice replied.

Halliday glanced at the handset once again, as if he could possibly have called any other number. "Sammy? Where's Sammy? Wh..Who is this?" he stuttered.

"Professor, my name is Officer Harrison. Ordinarily, it is not protocol to answer a discarded handset gathered as possible evidence at the scene of a terrorist attack, however..."

"Where's Sammy?" Halliday barked.

"...However Professor, you're clearly making your mark in this city and I'm keen to do the same. Sometime in the next twenty four hours they're going to want to bring you in for questioning. I've got my hands tied here at the scene till the small hours, I'm sure. Can you meet me at the university in the A.M. Professor? I want to get a jump on the suits that are gonna be headed your way." Harrison's tone hadn't changed, he continued, "Answering this cell phone Professor, could blow up in my face, if you catch my meaning – I mean, liaising with a suspected terrorist and all…"

"Terrorist?" a visibly rocked Halliday gulped.

"It's what the suits'll say. I'm obliged by the law to hand this cell in, and Professor I will – only, it's up to you on whether you wanna take a chance and meet with *me* or do this downtown." Harrison waited.

"Why should I trust you, how do I even know you are who you say you are? Oh, for the Gods, where's Sammy? This is absurd!" Halliday started shaking.

"Uni - the A.M. Professor?" Harrison urged.

"I've got a full programme pencilled for tomorrow at the university, I'm *expected* there!" Halliday blurted mockingly.

"I'll answer what I can for you but you gotta be straight with me or it's my ass too, you hear me? Get some sleep Professor, it could be a long day tomorrow." Harrison hung up and the Professor felt dizzy as he slumped back down on to his chair.

22

Dawn was breaking, and Hannah's tired body felt like it was breaking too after waking up a few blocks from anywhere remotely resembling familiarity. Although partially hidden from the elements beneath the rotten wooded struts that bridged Union Canal, her leggings were wet through and she her joints creaked as she stretched away the possibility of it all being a very bad dream. To confound her misery, she cursed aloud at the sight of an empty tobacco tin. "Not the best start to the day," she sighed, rolling her eyes with irony.

She looked over the flyer once again, wondering if the poor old boy who gave it her had had a better night's sleep than she did. "Okay L.C., this had better be good!", she said, thinking about having to face the inevitability of going back to university, unnoticed, but there was one more place she had to go first – if only she still had a key.

The streets were beginning to come alive with the sound of unhappy commuters exchanging angry bursts of car horns, making their way to monotonous, soul destroying day jobs around her. The rain had eased to a trickle but Hannah paced nimbly along the sidewalk with her heavy cargo jacket hood pulled low over her brow. Checking her stride, she pulled up alongside a news stand and waded through empty pockets trying to muster enough change for a packet of cigarettes. "Gimme a break!" she hissed empty handed and froze with terror. Her heart skipped a beat and she swallowed dryly, rooted to the spot. Hannah was literally staring back at herself. Every newspaper on the entire stand, bar the 'Sports In Short', had run a story on the previous night's events outside City Hall. Hannah's picture was emblazoned on every front cover and entitled as an accomplice to 'The Green Bomber'. Sammy was seen pictured clutching a red duffel bag with no doubting what was inside. The large print described Sammy an extremist, a cold blooded killer! Hannah stooped on bended knee, trying to take in what she was reading and shielding her face from view. Her eyes welled with tears as she read on. Sammy was dead, reported as 'taking her own life,' in an act of cowardice against the higher echelons of society, in some bizarre show of self-sacrifice gone awry! What the hell did that mean? Hannah thought - her face tight with anger. This was Sammy's rally sure, a peaceful demo – solely organised to raise the profile of the Professor's research and bring it to a wider audience. The Professor and assembled demonstrators were the good guys surely – none of this made any sense. Hannah swallowed dryly once again as the enormity of it all seeped in and the world slowly shrank around her.

The Professor had to be on to something surely, why else would this have ever taken place? Hannah knew Sammy, and she definitely knew she was no terrorist. Exhibitionist yes – terrorist, no!

"Excuse me, Missy? You browse it, you bought it!

That'll be...." The stand owner was saying, as Hannah sped off towards Alex's apartment block – crashing wildly through the ever growing throng of human cattle who seemed to graze in the dirty, rain-lashed, streets.

23

A blacked out official looking vehicle, a little too upmarket for this side of the city, pulled slowly into the morning traffic and melted into insignificance as it passed her.

Hannah crossed the street glancing upwards at the heavily misted sashes of Alex's apartment block. She felt sick as she climbed the slippery moss covered steps to the building lobby and tried to suppress the mixture of butterflies and anger that were rising within her.

"Be cool!", she told herself. She needed the rat bastard right now and the attention of a raging domestic on the door step had to be avoided at all costs. As crazy as it still sounded to her, she was being hunted. Her face would be broadcast on every bleary breakfast-eyed television screen across the land. An argument just wouldn't do. Alex's apartment door was ajar and she checked across the hall for Taylor's front door. It was almost customary for these two gaming freaks to sit online all day, every day, and shout crass insults across the hallway between apartments at one another. She frowned, slightly puzzled. Taylor's door was closed and Alex's mail was uncollected, something didn't seem quite right. Hannah poked the door a little further open and quietly called after Alex... "Babe?", she said hesitantly.

Hannah gripped the empty tobacco tin in her damp pocket as she realised she was holding her breath. "Baby?", she exhaled more cautiously as she entered the property. There was an unfamiliar smell hanging in her nostrils and she felt her pulse rise, shuddering slightly. Sulphur possibly? She recognised the scene from the night before. The fast food cartons and wine glasses, one glass cupping her key. "Ally babe?" she called and tiptoed into the bedroom.

Hannah inhaled sharply but suppressed the need to shriek. Alex was face down on the bed, naked, only his calves hidden by starchy blood-spattered sheets, with a single gunshot wound trickling semi-congealed blood from the back of his head. As if frozen next to him, lay a heavily tattooed, partially covered, body of a woman –

with a single bullet hole in the middle of her forehead. Hannah leaned over the dead woman and was almost sick. She looked just like her! Even the close cropped hair matched her own. Shaking again, but certainly not from the cold, she collected her thoughts looking about the room, then back down to the lifeless forms on the bed before her. There was no time for sentiment as an overwhelming panic slowly rippled through her.

"Dead pretty!" she said sardonically, tearing off her damp leggings in exchange for Alex's discarded denims. She stuffed her shaggy cargo with tobacco and cigarette papers from Alex's bedside table and pulled open the middle draw. "Blondes have more fun, eh?" she jested, surprised at her own devilish humour as she took out a shoulder length wig and fitted it hastily over her prickly scalp. "I guess I'm about to find out!" she snapped at the lifeless corpse, leaving the bedroom in a hurry.

She was without her wallet and decided to pocket Alex's, it wasn't like he was going to miss it anytime soon and she made for the lobby - picking up Alex's favourite baseball cap and adjusting it over her now blonde locks. Hannah closed the door behind her and pulled out Professor Halliday's promotional flyer, instantly thinking of Sammy. Hannah checked her wristwatch, tapping the cold glass face and fretting. The university would be beginning lectures within the hour.

She had to find the Professor - and quick.

24

Officer Harrison pulled his patrol car into one of the university's numerous parking lots. Looking for a non-reserved allocation, he broke sharply spilling the hot remains of his overly sugared morning wake-up call, partially over the dash and his inside leg. "Ah, come on!" burst Harrison, hitting the top of his weathered steering wheel and fumbling for the window lever - but the skateboard and rider had already melted into the sea of students and disappeared. He discarded the plastic cup onto the seat across from him, and backed the patrol car into a vacant lot. He continued to wipe down the now sticky dash and reached across for the black leather bound case file, entitled Halliday, Leighton C.

Harrison pondered the image on the first page of the file. The Professor seemed to stare helplessly back at him, almost questioningly. "Terrorist?" Harrison smiled, "*terrified* more like."

Harrison had spent the small hours, after escaping the madness of City Hall, whiling through what felt like hundreds of old press clippings hailing the Professor both a genius and madman alike. Halliday was a kook for sure, but a killer? Something wasn't right. Harrison felt the butterflies in him rise. Captain Stacey had talked of running this guy down, an open and shut case – of promotions from within et cetera, et cetera. He glanced over at the cell phone once again concealed in the evidence bag, and played over the messages in his head and frowned. Harrison could feel the weight of his father's shadow growing heavier as he recalled, "Fuck this up, and it's not just your ass, kid!"

Exiting the patrol car Harrison saw the dark mocha stain on his groin and giggled to himself, lightening his mood a little. He clicked the fob on his key chain and the car beeped twice in quick succession. He tucked the evidence bag inside his jacket and made for the university entrance across the parking lot.

Harrison hated technology and found himself growing increasingly frustrated with the university check-in system. There was more than one terminal but a small queue had already built-up behind him, as students signed in to classes hoping to better their prospective futures.

"C'mon stupid!" a mocking voice blurted beside him. Harrison swiveled on his heel, and the smile disappeared from the freckled student as he glimpsed the pistol hilt and badge. "Toilets are that away officer," he grinned, nodding towards the patch of drying coffee.

"Smart ass!" Harrison accused, zipping the bottom of his jacket. "Professor Halliday? Where does he lecture?" he pushed.

"Bomb sites mostly! C'mon!" rapped an unseen voice. The small group erupted with laughter. "The pyram-idiot's based in Block C, West, across the yard – can we sign in already please?"

Harrison stepped aside. The students filed through and Harrison looked over the building plan plastered across a huge sheet of plexiglass in the center of the foyer. Block C, West, was the other side of the university campus, and Harrison kissed his lips and shook his head, smiling at the irony - it had to be the furthest away didn't it!

Professor Halliday was in the midst of cancelling his morning classes when there was a stiff knock at his office door. The door opened without invitation and a handsome fresh-faced young man in a police issue trench coat entered the room.

Halliday put down his telephone receiver and asked, rather put out, "Can I help you, sir?"

"You can help yourself, Professor. I'm Officer Harrison, we spoke briefly last night after…" Harrison cocked his head, "you know, your firework display?"

"Okay, enough already officer. Firework display!? Oh please, c'mon! We may as well go straight downtown and I want my lawyer!" the Professor blasted.

"Okay Doc, I'm sorry - listen."

"I'm not a bloody Doctorate!" Halliday wheezed.

"I'm sorry," Harrison continued. "I do not know why Doc but," the Professor rolled his eyes sarcastically, "I'm on your team, okay?"

"On my team? I didn't even know there were bloody sides, officer!" Halliday began to shake nervously.

"Got the morning's papers?" Harrison started, slapping a copy of the Echo onto the desk. Halliday jumped a little. "Apparently, you're some kind of crank, a crazy geologist who's hell bent on disproving written history. Oh, and who repeatedly questions the motives of those in power whom make the decisions which set the course of history!"

"I get the picture officer, but..."

"Get the picture? Look at the picture, Doc!" Harrison was stabbing at the paper. Sammy was printed, straining to hold onto a red duffel bag and Halliday's eyes welled up a little.

"Sammy, where is she? Is she downtown?" Halliday asked, his eyes lighting from inside.

"Professor," Harrison hesitated. "Professor, I'm sorry - but this young lady is dead!"

25

A blacked out vehicle rolled slowly to a halt in the university parking lot. A broad-shouldered man in a black suit stepped out from the automobile, adjusted his cuffs and cracked his tight neck. He checked for his pistol glancing inside of his suit jacket and buttoned it once. The large man's chiseled and weathered features scowled as he noted the black and white parked across the lot. He made a mental note of the plate, instinctually more than anything else, and he set off toward four giant stone pillars, marking the entrance to one of the city's more famed universities. Standing in the shadow of the second pillar, the giant man pulled a cell phone from his pocket and hit redial.

Eyes hidden by mirrored shades, he surveyed the area for possible exits as he waited for the line to connect.

Hannah stubbed the remains of a long burned out cigarette with the heel of her boot. She shuddered a little at the vague memory of someone whom she couldn't place quite yet, as he strode away from the police unit parked across the lot. Pulling the peak of Alex's baseball cap down a little lower, Hannah followed the large man and stopped at the base of the university steps. She scratched at the back of her itching hairpiece and looked to roll another cigarette, as not to draw attention to herself.

"Is it done?" scoffed the Fat Man's voice, with a hint of self-satisfaction. "Well?"

"Sir, no sir. There is a police unit parked in the lot, our intel was that this guy was to be shaken down later in the day – they're already here, sir!" Neville's tone was as cold as it was harsh.

"You're not questioning the reliability of my source are you, Agent Neville? I can assure you that this police unit is not a matter of coincidence. Our people downtown have been instructed to place a hand selected greenhorn for the case. Now, the Professor's diary, Agent! Do not return without it! And be certain that there is no doubt that this is to be seen as nothing more than an unfortunate accident – a suicide maybe?" the Fat Man wheezed and disconnected the call.

Hannah's pulse quickened as she stole a glance at the man only metres away.

"Ma'am!" the burly man greeted as he turned away, sliding a metallic looking cell phone into his pocket. Hannah rocked visibly. He was clearly missing a finger.

Hannah felt bile rise in her mouth as she pictured this hulk of a man once again pushing a large digit-less hand into her face, before a bright burst of light and…

He was gone. Hannah dropped the partially rolled cigarette paper to the floor, fumbled for the tatty flyer in her cargo pocket and familiarised herself once again with the Professor's dashing features.

She knew the campus well enough to know that Halliday's office would be located somewhere on the far side of the many university halls and corridors and wasted no time in clambering up the steep masonry work and onto the premises, undetected.

26

Professor Halliday had spent the past fifteen minutes explaining, in stuttering detail, the events of the previous evening to the anxious officer seated across from him.

The officer was almost hidden from view, for the mountain of literature stacked precariously, resembling a city skyline on the desk space between them. A small picture of Sammy was framed amid the chaos of the old oak desktop. She was laughing playfully, whilst being carried on the back of a childhood friend wearing an over-sized badly fitting baseball cap, clearly not her own. Halliday stared vacantly at the image, still trying to come to terms with what he had learned from the officer present. It seemed the press had reported the blast as a coup gone wrong, the intended targets located within City Hall. Halliday had been systematically linked to the bomber in a thwarted attempt at the lives of the city's energy brokers in attendance. He had been likened to a classic movie villain, in some vain attempt at triggering some kind of new age revolution against the government. It was madness. Halliday brushed the hair of his wavy fringe from the line of his spectacles and drew a long breath.

"As absurd a question this may seem, officer. Are you here to take me in? I mean, I'm clearly on the verge of world domination, offering eye opening lectures to…" the Professor trailed off, feeling like he'd been hit by a train. "Oh, my word," he started, gripping the leather arm of his recliner. "I was right!" Halliday looked terrified, any remaining colour clearly draining from his already paled face.

"Doc?" Harrison offered leaning forward spilling a short stack of haphazardly stacked history books.

"It's happening again!" Halliday snapped, swiping his specs clear of his face and wiped his eyes, as if to see things a little clearer. "Oh shit, I should have seen this coming! Officer, we're in danger! We're all in terrible danger!"

"Okay Doc, calm down. I passed a coffee machine down the hall on my way over. You take sugar?" Harrison began to stand and the Professor just shook his shaggy head. "We're on the same team, remember? Gimme a minute and we'll go over this from the top. Don't take any calls, I'll be right back." Harrison closed the door behind him and walked briskly down the corridor, following the scent of cheap morning coffee.

27

Hannah sped blindly around one of the many brightly colour coded corners of C Block West, and skidded directly into the path of an unsuspecting coffee vending patron.

"My bad!" was all that Hannah offered, adjusting Alex's cap once more before taking off again at speed. Officer Harrison stopped short of cursing, and shook his fingers free of the hot freshly spilled coffee. Glancing again at the stain from earlier, he smiled and set the plastic cups down on top of the machine and crossed the hall for the restroom.

Hannah's heart was pounding inside her chest. The agent couldn't be far behind. The lecture rooms of the block were still empty as she rushed by the large circular windows resembling the riveted portholes of a holiday cruise liner.

"C'mon, where the…?" she stammered. She caught sight of what looked to be some kind of family tree, webbing together a mesh of odd featured lecturers in badly fitting garments, plastered across the whitewashed walls. She skidded past as she tried to come to a stop, nearly ripping the whole montage from the wall itself. Hannah drew a frantic invisible line with her finger, slalom-like down the wall plan, dismissing the numerous smug looking faces staring back at her. She was breathing heavily and trying to regain some composure. Professor L.C. Halliday, with his fuzzy mop of hair and wire-rimmed glasses smiled reluctantly away from the camera. Printed beneath, somewhat like a mugshot mock-up, Hannah reflected, was Geology Block, Room 101.

"L.C.," Hannah confirmed, stiffly prodding the Professor's likeness beneath her finger. This was Geology, and 101 couldn't be far, she was sure. She took off again, dancing round a couple of students engrossed in conversation in the ever busying hallway. "Ninety one, ninety two..." Hannah counted aloud as she sped by the vacant rooms, peering inside each one as best she could. "101!" Hannah glanced back down the hallway. Half a dozen students, at best, were milling around the end of the corridor and there was no sign of the agent. Not yet. She drew a deep breath, and taking the door by the handle leaned inside.

"Okay officer," Halliday began. He was hunched over heavily and tenderly pawing at a cheap looking photo frame in his hands.

"Officer!?" Hannah started, immediately jumping a little and checking the hallway again, instinctively.

The Professor shifted in his seat weighing up the impromptu entrance of his new guest and half-cleared his throat before announcing, "Dr Kusevra," pausing and rolling his eyes, "can be found in the very same lecture hall he has resided in ever since…"

"Not now L.C.!" a hint of panic in Hannah's voice.

"Halliday, yeah?" she'd closed the door behind her and was flicking at the blinds as the Professor sat pale-faced and bemused. He brushed his line of sight free from his hair and leaned forward, "I'm sorry, but I think you may have the wrong…"

Hannah shrieked above him her eyes wild, "No games Professor, what the fuck is going on!?" no sooner had she left them, Hannah was back at the window peeking through the dust drenched blinds again. Turning on him she continued, "I'm fucking dead! They *think* I'm fucking dead! Alex's dead. And Sammy, oh Sammy what the fuck is happening, what have you done!?"

"Sammy!" Halliday exclaimed. "Who the hell are you and what do you know of..?" he glanced back to the picture frame in his clammy palms.

"She said that 'you were right all along' Professor, right before the…" Hannah trailed off dashing to the window once more.

"Before? Before what? Who did you say you are?" Halliday was clearly rattled now and an element of fear rose inside him.

"The explosion, Professor! I saw it. I saw… him!" Hannah's eyes widened with recollection. She bolted from the blinds in panic. "He's here! We've got to get out of here. The man with the hand, he's…!"

"What man? What hand? You mentioned Sammy!" Halliday stared back into the picture frame in his hands, and quickly back at the intruder. "Spam?" he offered enquiringly.

Hannah's ears pricked at the sound of Sammy pet name for her.

"I don't know what you were right about L.C., but we gotta get outta here, like yesterday!" Fingering the blind she momentarily froze with terror. A large man in an out of place suit and tinted shades strode briskly down the narrow corridor, and peered into the first circular window at the head of the corridor.

Hannah cast her gaze past the Professor's door and to the other end of the corridor. There were three, maybe four more lecture rooms and a fire escape. Her heart sank at the idea of escape being only footsteps away and not being able to reach it. The Professor was mumbling something frantically flicking through an old weathered leather binder but Hannah wasn't listening. "There's got to be another way out!" pushing past Halliday, Hannah wrenched open the double doors that stood behind him. An old glass heat stained beaker lazily bounced off of the peak of Hannah's baseball cap, and crashed in to pieces on the polished floor at her feet.

Agent Neville stiffened adjusting his line of vision down the hall and patting his jacket for confirmation of his pistol.

"L.C.? Professor? Is there another exit?" she hissed through clenched teeth.

There was another door across the room obscured by a heavy looking raincoat and over-sized scarfs. The Professor was gesturing towards it. "It links mine, Dr Kusevra and…" Halliday was yanked from his leather rooting and was ushered rather awkwardly through the doorway. The Professor, at a crouch, walked straight into Hannah who spun round and clasped a hand over his mouth. Agent Neville's cold silhouette slowly passed the first of the office's two small portholes eyeing the interior. Hannah yanked her companion by the sleeve as they clung low to the walls, inching their way silently across the lecture room. The footsteps in the hallway stopped. Hannah and the Professor held their paths and their breath. Hannah was perched directly beneath the second of the two windows and silently motioned to the Professor. Neville squinted through his sunglasses and strained his eyes staring into the gloom within. The door from which they had entered clicked shut on the far side of the room. Neville took Dr Kusevra's door by the handle and pulled down. Hannah watched terrified as the brass handle on her side of the heavy door almost brushed against her face. The agent unbuttoned his jacked and felt for the cold steel of his pistol. He leaned onto the door with a firm shoulder and grunted. The door was locked. Neville scowled and released his grip of the handle and his firearm and headed directly towards Room 101 a few metres down the hallway. Professor Halliday exhaled blowing his mop from his face and smiled, silently offering Hannah some gum. Hannah raised a reproachful eyebrow and pulled him in tow. The link door for this particular office was locked but Halliday had produced a key from his musty suit jacket, and they slipped through. "L.C.!" Hannah grimaced at the Professor as she watched him take the time to lock his colleague's lecture hall before leaving the Geology Block behind them.

Agent Neville coolly ran the knuckle of a deformed hand across the highly polished brass name plaque, adjacent door 101. Professor L.C. Halliday. Dead eyes beneath his sunglasses stole a look back up the hallway. The corridor was clear. Neville's good hand slipped inside his jacket feeling for the pistol hilt, while he cranked the handle and stepped gingerly into the darkened room. The blinds were drawn and broken glass crunched into the tread of his boots, under his heavy step. The faint scent of a woman, somewhat reminiscent of the young couple's apartment he'd occupied earlier that morning, alerted his trained senses. The bitch was dead, he snorted to himself. Neville shook it from his mind and surveyed the Professor's office. Pictures of archaeological dig sites and relics alike adorned the office walls, including ancient maps of the world with unfamiliar looking coastlines not depicted on anything he'd seen before. His attention was drawn to the far side of the room. There appeared to be a web of interconnecting string, pinned chaotically across a whiteboard of high powered political figures and world energy leaders. Amongst the mayhem were pictures of constellations and depleted rainforests. None of which made any sense to him, except for one. A single thread of the string drew down and away from everything else. A solitary picture, obviously ripped from some kind of geological magazine, was tacked to the whiteboard. Neville had seen this image before and tapped it knowingly. He replaced his pistol and reached for his phone, unlocked it and hit speed dial.

"It will be reported as an accident?" proffered the Fat Man almost delightfully on the end of the line.

Neville braced himself. "Sir, the target is no longer on site. There's a black and white in the lot but I'm..."

"He's alive?" the Fat Man scoffed, now sounding a little distraught.

"Sir, the situation…" Neville asserted.

"The situation is unacceptable!" the Fat Man reprimanded. "Find him, find him now, I want that journal!"

"I think the target could well come to us sir…" The line disconnected. Agent Neville snatched at the image from the whiteboard and left the room.

28

Officer Harrison exited the restroom still drying his damp fingers on a paper towel, and picked up the slightly cooled coffee cups from the vending machine.

"Morning!" Harrison offered, as a rather large yet unusually official looking gentleman strode past him in the corridor. The man nodded discreetly without reply and kept walking. "Yeah, have a nice day!" Harrison continued, under his breath smiling to himself. Turning back down the hall he noticed what appeared to be splinters of glass, the artificial light above him reflecting on their jagged edges, peppered intermittently down the narrow passageway. A little puzzled, he stole a look back up the hallway and sipped at his coffee. The hallway was empty. Butterflies began to arise in the pit of his stomach and he swore out loud for being stupid enough to leave the Professor unattended. Harrison broke into a light jog, trying in vain not to spill anymore coffee. Recalling that he had closed the door to Room 101 behind him, his eyes widened as he saw the Professor's door was ajar and glass filings scattered randomly at the threshold. The blinds were drawn too. Setting the lukewarm beverages down at his feet, he coolly drew his sidearm and pushed the door open with the barrel.

"Professor?" Harrison paused. "Professor Halliday?"

A large red bell rang out in short bursts above the doorway, signalling the start of the day on campus. Harrison jumped nervously as if it were gunfire and swiped at the fresh beads of sweat now breaking on his forehead. "Professor Halliday, you in there?". There was no answer. Staying low, Harrison rolled his shoulder blades on the frame of the door and entered the room, gun levelled. Glass crunched under foot and he swung his weapon towards every corner of the office space, eliminating potential threats from within. The Professor was gone and the room was empty. Harrison's cheeks puffed as he exhaled violently and got back to his feet. There was glass everywhere and he kicked it aside as he groped at the blinds, shedding better light on the situation. Other than the shard strewn floor, everything else in the room was as Harrison had left it only minutes before. There was a door in the corner of the office he hadn't seen before and he cranked the handle and leaned in.

"Professor?"

Hitting the lights, he saw the lecture hall was empty and made his way across the room towards the only other exit. It was locked. Harrison shook his head in frustration and re-entered Halliday's office. He took out his cell phone, unlocking it with a swipe of his thumb, and snapped a number of camera shots at the labyrinth of string and images plastered across the wall. He stepped out of the office briefly, only to return with a half-filled plastic cup. Finishing the coffee, Harrison sat at the Professor's desk and rooted through the fine oak draws, eventually slouching back, empty-handed, into the leather recliner to ponder his next move. Frustrated, he grabbed the empty drinking vessel, screwed it up, and launched it at a picture of the lecturer receiving some kind of award, which was perched on the edge of the desk. Harrison cocked his head and questioned what he was looking at. There was another picture frame on the highly polished work place. This one was face down. Harrison was certain this wasn't the case when he had entered to the office earlier that morning and sat back up sliding it towards him. Staring back at him was the girl from the vending machine collision only moments before, still sporting the over-sized baseball cap and grinning from ear to ear with the same girl from this morning's newspapers.

29

Hannah sat across from the Professor, at an annoyingly sticky, beverage stained, table, in the back of a dimly lit café in Central Station. It was a master stroke as far as she was concerned. Yes, they were fugitives, or at least as far as the Professor was concerned anyway. She would now be presumed dead she thought to herself reflecting on the time spent at Alex's apartment. Yet hiding out in one of the busiest places in the entire city, where nobody paid the blindest piece of attention to anything other than their destination, was genius. But Halliday had other ideas.

Commuters, in their thousands, shuffled past, outside the cafeteria. They offered muted apologies to one another and grimaces alike, as they jostled for position at platform turn-style bottlenecks, all blissfully unaware that the city's most wanted were sipping bitterly cheap coffee in their midst.

"Professor?" said Hannah, eagerly, tugging at Halliday's crumpled sleeve. "Professor?" she persisted, clenching her teeth and shaking him from his daydream.

"I'm sorry, it's just..." Halliday paused and seemed to drift off again, wrapped up in his own thoughts and despair.

"L.C.!" she snapped, and shunted to table a little towards him, spilling yet more overly sugared liquid onto the table's surface and the Professor's fingers. Halliday shifted in his seat as if an electrical charge had pulsed through his entire body and winced.

"Sammy? Sam?" Halliday searched, almost looking through Hannah and beyond. Hannah relaxed a little at the sound of her friend's name, but more so at the semi-amusing sight of Professor Halliday craning his neck in all directions – not unlike the native pigeons that clung to the rafters above in this ageing, dirt-ridden station, she mused.

"Sammy's…gone, Professor!" Hannah's eyes saddened, along with the Professor's. She let out a long sigh and slumped backwards. This time Halliday leaned forward and clasped the teenager's warm hands in his own.

"I'm scared too, Spam." he started. Hannah smiled warmly at him, pulling away to wipe at her glazed eyes with a frayed sleeve.

"Didn't think I'd hear that name again." she sniffed

quietly.

"Hmmm, you meant the world to her you know? Spam this, Hannah that. Always relating a situation, 'Spam wouldn't have it!' she'd say." Halliday chuckled to himself.

"Professor," she began, reaching for the security of his grip again. "She said that you were right all along. 'L.C. was right!' she said. Right about what, exactly? What did she mean?"

"It's a long story." Halliday looked almost embarrassed. "Longer than history would have you believe," he said shaking his head.

"What the hell does that mean?" Hannah asserted, pulling herself up.

Halliday looked a little more focused now. "We've been lied to Hannah. For hundreds of years, thousands if you really think about it, I mean…"

"What *do* you *mean*?" she pressed urgently before he rallied off on another tangent.

"Yes, of course. Sorry, sometimes I can get a little… erm..."

"Professor?" Hannah gestured tipping her head and

raising her eyebrows mockingly.

Halliday cleared his throat. Reaching inside his weathered leather satchel he produced an even older looking diary and began flicking through the tatty pages thoughtfully. "Fuel! Energy! Power!" he exclaimed. He stopped on a page which had been taped back into the journal, from obvious overuse. The Professor was stabbing the remnants of a well chewed index fingernail on the image in front of them both. "We're destroying ourselves," he continued. "The finite resources of this beautiful planet are almost at an end. We have become the masters of our own demise. We've reached a technological age in which everything, and I do mean everything, relies solely on the means to power it. Energy. We need energy, and we're running out!" Halliday swept a hand through his hair and inhaled deeply. "The fossil fuels mined for the past century or so, needed to run and maintain uncountable power stations around the world are almost at an end! We need fuel to produce food, the most basic of human requirements, surely? Without an alternative means of creating energy, the planet will starve. These same government controlled energy companies are apparently, we are told, spending untold riches in order to produce an alternative source of worldwide energy."

"So, what's the problem?" Hannah looked at a loss.

"I believe we've already found it!" he almost looked smug, smiling back at her.

"Meaning?..." she lingered.

"Meaning Hannah, that the powers that be, already know about this alternative means of energy and are destroying the planet regardless!" his voice was growing louder. "The masses, including yourself and I, have been spoon-fed a fictitious path throughout history, for the past few centuries at least! The ancients of prehistory have been robbed of a glorious technological advancement, which has been purposefully hidden from us! We don't need to drain the planet in order to feed humankind anymore, we *never* had to - which is precisely my point!"

A polite voice offered a refill beside them. Both declining, Halliday checked his notes as the waitress disappeared.

"What's with the pyramid?" Hannah questioned, staring down at the leather bound image in front of her. There was what appeared to be a bolt of lightning striking the apex of the pyramid, drawn in fading pencil. Overlaid the rough edges of the pyramid's sides were a handful of chemical symbols she should have recognised, but couldn't recall. "I didn't make many history or physics classes Professor. Not sure I follow, sorry."

"That's just it! History is wrong, you're not meant to follow!" he wailed. Hannah could see a marked change in the Professor's persona, his passion was uncontained. He'd lit up like the tiniest of flames in the darkest of rooms. "They'll have history as they want *you*, *me*, *everyone* to believe it! Just because it's written, doesn't make it so! The world was flat only a few hundred years ago, think about it!" Hannah almost cut in - worried he would stray from the point once again but swallowed her words before they surfaced. His enthusiasm was inspiring and she was beginning to understand Sammy's attraction to him.

"Who writes history anyway?" Halliday asked. "Those empowered to, that's bloody well who!" he continued, not waiting for an answer. "Walk into any classroom the world over and they are teaching the future generations what they want to be believed and not that which is true! Again, if you have the tenacity to question the teachings, you are once again collectively ridiculed by your peers. Should anyone challenge the path of history as we know it, they, like I, are labelled a crackpot and publically ridiculed and shamed. It's a cycle. Can't you see? It's not in their interest to go public and put their hands up in front of the world and say, 'Oh, by the way, we no longer care for the control of the world economy and the monstrous profiteering at the expense of the planets dwindling, life supporting resources, and we are happy to announce there is a better way and you don't need us lot anymore, thank you and goodbye!'" his sarcasm *more* than evident.

Hannah felt the world close in tightly around her, and she found herself steeling glances over her shoulder at the enormity of what she was hearing, in case anyone else was listening. She'd felt unsafe before they had even sat down but now she could feel her stomach twisting inside and she loosened her heavy cargo feeling a little paranoid.

There was a muffled intermittent vibrating coming from the Professor's pocket. He reached inside and retrieved a glowing cell phone which read: Sammy. Hannah stiffened as if she'd seen a ghost and pushed Halliday's hands away. The Professor, though, knew who was on the end of the line but ignored it deciding to explain the situation to the grief stricken face in front of him. "Hey now, I know, I know. It's okay. Look..." he paused, realising how this would sound but continued regardless. "Officer Harrison, the police officer from the university this morning. He found Sammy's cell phone outside City Hall last night. I think he's okay, you know. *He* tipped me about them wanting to bring me in for questioning et cetera. Yeah sure, he's working for the people who are looking for us, but I think this guy could help *us*!" He paused. "Maybe?" Halliday was clearly fishing for support.

"Doc, are you out of your mind?" Hannah insulted.

"I'm not a... oh nevermind!" Halliday shook his head.

The cell phone stopped its vibrating dance solo across the table and fell silent. Both went mute, first looking at the discarded cell and then at each other. They both went to talk when the cell phone came alive once more: Sammy, blinked the screen. Hannah snatched up the phone and connected the call. The sound of empty coffee cups being collected and the crash of a cash register could be heard, as a muffled but authoritive voice boomed out various train cancellations as she placed it to her ear.

"Hello?" She said softly.

"Hello Hannah," came the reply.

Shaken, Hannah recoiled and glared at the cell phone and then the Professor. "How the fuck…?"

"Slow down Missy, slow down," Harrison broke in. "I'd have said the same thing earlier, if you'd have given me the chance. You owe me a coffee, lady."

Her mind's eye recalled the collision in the Geology Block corridor.

"He's got four fingers!" stated Hannah, under her breath.

"Excuse me?" Harrison said.

"Yes, you're right!" she replied. "I should've said..., sorry, excuse me!"

There was a beeping sound in Hannah's ear and she glanced at the cell. The battery was low.

Placing it back to her ear, Officer Harrison was talking about not doing anything stupid or something to that effect.

"Anything stupid?" Hannah laughed loudly. "Like getting as far a-fucking-way as possible and trying to stay alive? That said, I'm already dead aren't I, officer!?" she jested sarcastically. The Professor just looked out of the window, twisting his shaggy hair around his finger like a child watching the pigeons. The train cancellation was repeated, but louder this time, as a rather wet looking commuter swept the door open at the front of the café, brushing himself down at the counter.

"Hannah, you can trust me. My ass is on the line just

talking to you. If the Capo knew I had this cell he'd probably charge me for perverting the course of justice! Your friend's phone is crime scene evidence, you understand! I was hedging my bets the press were wrong. Or, maybe, I'm wrong?"

The cell phone beeped once more, this time a little dimmer.

"Officer," Hannah started.

"Call me Hayden," he said reassuringly.

"Listen Mister, I don't know who to fucking trust anymore! Police officers? Professors? Fuel cells, prison cells? It's all the same to me right now! All I know for sure is..." The call disconnected. Hannah looked at the phone in her hand. The battery was dead and she slapped it back on the table, making the Professor jump.

"That went well!" Halliday chirped.

Hannah rolled a cigarette in frustrated silence while the Professor looked on. Picking up the discarded phone, he smiled before adding, "C'mon, we've got a train to catch!"

30

Officer Harrison gave an affirmative smile at recalling his muted joy after hearing the train cancellation, in conversation with the fugitive. He'd spent the past hour upstairs in Grand Central Station's CCTV monitoring rooms, playing back grainy real time images hoping to get lucky. The plucky young camera operator next to him couldn't have been more disinterested, instead offering only short lived fantasies to certain, mostly female, commuters and their possible destinations. Harrison loosened his neck tie and fretted inwardly. He was adjusting the focus on one of the dozen or so levers on a vast control panel, which would not have looked out of place in a space station – let alone a train station.

"Take it back!" exclaimed Harrison suddenly.

The operator jumped in his seat, his feet flailing in the air trying to keep balance as he rocked back and forth.

"Take it back, now!"

"What did I say?" the operator looked stumped. "C'mon, Chief. It's not like she can hear me right?" He sat forward taking a large bite of cold pizza, smiling contently as he chewed.

Harrison was shaking his head. "The video you idiot, take it back!"

"The video? Sure, sure, the video!" wiping his lips with his free hand, he played back the last twenty seconds of footage and offered Harrison a beaten looking pizza box.

Harrison refused with a silent shake of his head, and peered into the monitor. "There! Right there!"

The op paused the sequence and pulled it back a few frames, adjusting a handful of dials on the over-elaborate control panel. The grainy image on screen slowly cleared, as if the realisation of what was thought to be a mirage actually materialised before them. Harrison's face lit up. The screenshot was no longer distorted. A pale young lady sporting an ill-fitting blue baseball cap and cargo jacket, was frozen in obvious conversation with a wiry looking gentleman exiting a platform coffee house.

"Bingo!" he punched the air, self-assured.

"Not bad Chief, very nice if do say so myself!" the operator shot Harrison a casual wink.

"Knock it off and play the tape. You can follow them, right?" Harrison pressed.

"That's why they pay me!" the operator beamed, pulling himself into position. The video feed continued. The operator hastily got to work, shifting from one screen to the next. Harrison lost his fugitives twice, trying to make sense of the vast starship control panel the op eagerly tweaked and nudged with greasy fingers. Harrison was becoming frustrated at not being able to keep up.

"All aboard!" the operator bellowed and kicked back his chair thumping his feet back on the desktop. A five second loop played over and over, hazily but in real time. Hannah and the Professor were seen boarding a train and disappearing from view.

Harrison clapped the op on the shoulder exclaiming his genius, but the op just tried not choke on a fresh mouthful of pizza and smiled through his coughing.

"What's the destination? Where's it headed?" Harrison was clearly still in a hurry and trying to make out what he could of the images on screen, without much success. "And get me on the next train!" he added.

"Why not this one?" smacked the op's greasy lips through a mouthful of cold dough.

"What did you say?"

"Why not *this* train? It's sat idle for the past two hours but leaves in…" he paused checking the timetable against his wristwatch. "Three minutes!"

"It's still *here*?" Harrison looked confused.

"Sure, just about. How many times a day d'ya think the Intercontinental Expressway runs a service? Not much call for where they're going!" The reply was more sarcastic than informative.

Harrison grabbed his jacket, which had been lazily slumped over the back of his chair and bolted for the exit.

The camera operator, looking rather pleased with himself, hollered in Harrison's general direction, "Platform 13... and you're gonna need sunscreen!"

31

The Fat Man chewed a burnt out cigar, rolling it from one side of his mouth to the other. He stood lost in his own thoughts, staring at his reflection from the glass casing that housed one of a number of ancient artefacts that adorned his high-rise office. The office itself was based in the banking district of the city, as a symbol of power perched high above the dirty streets below. The company logo was emblazoned on the back wall behind the energy magnate's over-sized desktop, a fearsome lion, sitting proud and at rest - its mane shimmering gold from which it was cast. Arched above the feline silhouette sat the company name, E.M. POWER.

An intercom buzzed, its little red LED pulsing gently atop the marble desktop. The Fat Man squinted through his monocle as he turned from the wall mounted relic and paced towards the marble feature, wheezing as his cane bowed beneath him. A chubby, well-manicured finger accepted the call and the buzzing ceased.

"Send him in!" the Fat Man grunted, and sat heavily in his seat.

Agent Neville entered the room placing his mirrored sun glasses into his jacket pocket and stood at the apex of the triangular shaped table, as the Fat Man greeted him with a piercing stare.

"Report!" Fat Man scoffed, pouring a large alcoholic drink into a fine crystal glass and reached for his lighter.

Neville faced forward not attempting to sit down and spoke directly into the glistening monocle. "Sir, as yet I do not believe the target has acquired 'The Key'. He has left the city and is believed to be heading back to the original dig site. There is only one reason he would be stupid enough to return."

The Fat Man snorted and put a flame to his cigar. Neville continued, "The Professor *will* be deleted, this I assure you. Only, I believe the fool is going to lead us to the key first and then 'the build' can continue on schedule. He has the journal with him!"

The Fat Man exhaled a large plume of smoke and coughed as he spoke. "The build can continue?" his gaze piercing the smog. "What do you assume to know of the build?" he enquired.

"Sir?" Neville offered.

"The build Agent Neville, what do you suppose to know of it?" the Fat Man's face reddened.

"I-I don't understand, sir!"

"Good Neville, understanding can be a very dangerous thing!" he sucked on the cigar. "Our dear Professor has claimed to 'understand' and he will soon be dead! I'm sure *you* understand!" the Fat Man smiled smugly. He rose from his leather recliner and walked around the table beckoning the agent to follow. "Come," he said.

The Fat Man brushed past the hulk nonchalantly and they made their way across the office space to the wall mounted glass casing the Fat Man was mulling over only moments before.

"My dear boy," the Fat Man started "do you suppose to understand what these are?" he gently tapped the protective glass shell with a giant lion-like ring which appeared to be embedded within his chubby finger. Behind the casing stood three conical granite artefacts, all of which were approximately twelve inches in height and rather curiously engraved. Before Neville could reply the Fat Man continued, pointing at the first of the encased relics. "A story, Agent Neville, of unimaginable power!" His eyes gleamed at the thought as he tapped at the outer casing with his cane as it scrolled across to the second. "It's an idea. Another way, you might say! We have *our* way, but there is another..." he paused, "more *profitable* way!" He shuffled sideways leaning on his cane and gestured towards the glass, clearly marking the last of the carvings from the others. "You see, the Professor isn't a *complete* crank Agent Neville, although it is how he will be remembered, I'm sure." He afforded himself a cold smile. "We cannot continue to plunder the planets natural resources as a means of energy at the expense of the planet itself, the Professor is correct, I have no doubt! Scientists across the globe are frantically trying to develop 'the new' fuel cell as they have for decades now. The creators of an alternative fuel cell could theoretically rule the world. They would have complete control! They would have *absolute* power!"

Neville's gaze gravitated towards the Fat Man as he straightened his broad shoulders and eased a knot in his neck. The Fat Man jerked his walking cane upwards with a snap of his wrist. The polished bamboo cane struck the underside of the glass casing with such a force that it splintered upon impact. Neville's gaze was re-averted. The Fat Man, using the cane so as not to cut himself on the jagged edges, cleared away the broken remains and reached inside, retrieving the granite artefact.

"The build," the Fat Man grunted caressing the carved relief, "would never have begun construction without a blue print!" he held the rough object aloft admiring it. "But of what good is an engine without the means to start it?" he snapped, warm spittle spraying the Agent's face as did the rancid stench of expensive stale cigars. Neville clenched his jaw as his fists tightened at his side. He stood fast.

The Fat Man hurled the relic across the room, shattering another elaborate looking display case and its priceless contents from antiquity. He padded his way back over to the desktop picking a path through the broken glass and squeezed into his recliner with a creek. Neville was still rooted to the spot.

"Agent Neville?" he bellowed. "It's about time we put

our disobedient little dog on a leash, don't you think? This charade has gone on long enough! I want the Professor's journal and if he doesn't have the information we require, then maybe he will indeed lead us to it!"

The Fat Man stabbed at the intercom once impatiently. "Ready the jet!"

32

Rain lashed against the cabin windows outside as the Intercontinental Expressway thundered out of the city, leaving metropolitan life far behind. Hannah returned from the restroom smelling of cigarette smoke and started whistling playfully, as she registered the obvious look of disapproval from the Professor.

"Anyway," Hannah started with a cheeky expression. "Are we there yet?"

Halliday chuckled. He could see where Sammy got her humour from and he dearly missed her reassurance at a time like this. "How long did you know her for? Sammy, I mean," he began.

Hannah's sprightliness diminished almost immediately

and she slumped against the window tucking her knees under her chin.

"I'm sorry," the Professor offered. Hannah smiled through glazed eyes, nodding wearily.

"She was like the sister I always wanted but never had." her gaze fixed on the Professor. "She's gone now though isn't she? Would she be? I mean, if not for you?" she unclasped her hands and leaned on the tiny table separating them. Halliday reeled back, shocked at the sudden change in the girl.

"I was just…"

"Just in the middle of explaining what kind of shit bomb you've exploded into my life, when officer 'You're dead and you owe me a coffee' called and I ended up a fugitive on this tin train to the tropics?" Hannah sat back and fumbled for her cigarettes once again.

Halliday didn't know where to look. He fidgeted nervously and straightened, then re-straightened his spectacles. "Well yes, erm, we were..." he retrieved his note book from inside his jacket. "We were... oh dear..." The Professor looked startled as Hannah snatched the tatty bound pages from his grasp and rifled through them feverishly until she was satisfied. Slapping it open face up on the table, she nudged it back in Halliday's general direction. The Professor glanced down at the image of the pyramid he had hand drawn on his original trip to the sub-continent, several months before.

"Yes, as I was saying!" he exclaimed.

"You were saying history is wrong, or something to that effect?" Hannah had relaxed a little, affording the Professor to continue unabated.

Halliday swept back his shaggy mop, scratching at his scalp and continued, "Nothing is quite what is seems, Hannah. History, that is. I have proposed, for some time now that the ancient 'undocumented' civilisations of this planet were far more technologically advanced than we ever dared give them credit for. Think about it!" he was stabbing at the open page Hannah had offered from his diary.

"These colossal megastructures, these pyramids are scattered haphazardly across the entire globe! Why?" he looked almost amused. "To lay to rest a King or Queen? *Please*!" he was certainly amused, his eyes bright with passion.

"And we are expected to believe these geometrically sound megaliths were created with nothing more than stones and copper chisels by a slave workforce? It's absurd! But therein lies the problem Hannah, that is what we have been taught, so that is precisely what we believe! We could create such monumental builds today yes, but only with the aid of current technological prowess! Stone cutting machinery and cranes et cetera, power tools! It's clearly evident that these ancient peoples had access to this kind of technology. They had to! And, of course, it had to be powered. They were masters of an alternate source of energy and I surmise that this was an ecologically sound source of energy and that they lived in relative harmony with their environment! That is until a violent cataclysm wiped them from the face of the planet." He frantically scratched through the pages.

"Cataclysm? How'd you mean?" Hannah was engrossed.

"Here, you see? Some thirteen thousand years ago, an undocumented path in human evolution, continuously open to debate, a comet struck the northern hemisphere of the planet! The impact of which would have been the equivalent of two or three thousand atomic bombs! They were doomed! Almost instantaneously the ice caps would have reached two thousand degrees! The ice-melt forming tsunamis perhaps a thousand feet high! Civilisation, no matter how advanced would not stand a chance. Sea levels rose overnight and submerged those closest to the coastline which were then forgotten, erased from history! Look, here!" The Professor flicked from one page to the next. The evidence of this cataclysm was becoming overwhelming. Pictures of impact zones, geologically sound man-made structures which were hundreds of metres below the current sea level! "Think about it! Most of the planet has been wiped out with the initial comet impact, nature's way of hitting the reset button if you like! Those whom survive, and surely a small number would, presumably those who do not live in the sprawling cities and know how to fend for themselves in the remotest parts of the planet - what would happen to them? Civilisation has been obliterated, and the comet fallout would have created a dust cloud large enough to envelop three quarters of the planet, lasting for centuries! This alone would cause famine and a new way of thinking! Survival of the fittest, I believe is *today's* terminology. De-evolution, if I may be so bold!"

"Devo, what?" said Hannah.

"De-evolution, my dear!" Halliday took off his jacket and rolled up his sleeves reaching for Hannah's lighter.

"I didn't think you...?" Hannah started.

"I don't!" the Professor smiled. "And nor possibly would you, without this! Tell me, can you make fire?"

"What?" Hannah looked baffled and snatched the lighter back.

"Okay, given the time you presumably would, you're an intelligent girl. But, my point being, *we* have come to rely on the lighter's convenience, have we not?"

"What's smoking got to do with anything?"

"It's a metaphor Hannah!" he shook his head. "Everything in today's society we take for granted! Your lighter, the cell phone, this bloody train! Do you know how any of it works? I mean, really? I don't, the lighter maybe okay, but come on think about it! If the knowledge of all of these things we take for granted just disappeared overnight, evolution would have reached its zenith and mankind would take one giant step backwards! Back to its roots, literally! De-evolution. Everything would have to be learned again. From the beginning! There would be no geologists, no doctors, scientists, teachers or anything. There would be no need for them at first either, because man's initial instinct would be to survive, to eat and find shelter and protect his family! Nothing would be documented because the evolved art of writing would, over a short period of time, become obsolete, there would not be a need for it! Man's sole concern being survival."

Hannah puffed her cheeks, blowing outwardly. "Heavy!" she blurted. "But what's with the pyramid?" She fumbled back to the original line of questioning.

Halliday sat a little straighter. "What *is* a pyramid?" he was looking over the wire frame of his specs.

"A tomb?" Hannah replied more in question than answer.

"And therein lies the lie!" he pushed the frames up the bridge of his nose.

"Here we go!" she sighed.

"Hannah, would any reasonably sane civilisation build a structure on this sort of scale, with the proposed stone and copper chisels at their disposal, or even with today's technological know-how, merely to bury their leader? The megastructure's interior is a labyrinth of precision cut passageways, described by scholars as burial chambers and booby traps for potential grave robbers! It sounds plausible but it's hilarious. In fact it is down-right ridiculous considering no mummified bodies have ever been found inside. Ever! Yet it is what we are taught! What we believe!"

"So, your overwhelming evidence against this chapter in history is what exactly?" Hannah poked. Halliday frowned accordingly.

"A geometrically sound pyramid," the Professor winced "is a power station!"

"A what?" Hannah laughed openly.

"Yes," he chuckled along with her "a power station!"

The Expressway shuddered as it leaned into a bend on the tracks and an almighty crack of lightening lit up the cabin, making Hannah jump.

"Here, let me explain!" Halliday was clearly excited, and moved from one booth to the other and sat down beside her. "First and foremost, the pyramid is constructed using a number of different stones! There is a reason for this, to which my point will gravitate towards, please bear with me! You must understand that over two million limestone blocks of various sizes have been quarried, cut and systematically placed beside and on top of one another so precisely that not even a razor blade or piece of paper may fit inbetween them!"

"Okay, cool!" agreed Hannah.

The Professor shot her a look of disapproval at such a nonchalant reply to this revelation but decided not to challenge her and continued to summarise.

"Limestone does not contain magnesium and has extremely high insulating properties. This would keep any source of electrical current housed inside the structure and keep it from being released or discharged without control. The massive blocks within the pyramid are of another type of limestone, containing crystal and small traces of base metals allowing maximum power transmission!"

"I'm with you so far but have I missed where this particular electrical current is coming from?" Hannah hoped the answer would be as straight forward as the question.

"All in good time Hannah, stay with me on this, okay?" The Professor was looking rather pleased with himself and Hannah went to light another cigarette. Another disapproving look followed the cigarette being almost swatted from Hannah's lips, "All in good time my dear!"

It was Hannah's turn to offer a look of disgust but the Professor had missed it and rattled on with his explanation regardless.

"The shafts inside the chambers are documented as being lined with granite. Granite is a conductor and a slightly radioactive substance which assists if not permits the ionization of the air inside these shafts!"

Hannah screwed up her face trying to take on-board the information and dispaired inwardly. She hated chemistry and the Professor could see she was struggling, deciding to break it down and simplify his theory. "Picture the cross-section of an everyday electrical wire, for instance.

The pyramid is constructed in much the same way, conductive materials on the inside – insulating materials on the outside."

Hannah winked playfully, "Why didn't you say that in the first place?"

"I believe I did." He pressed on with a smile. "As you correctly proposed a moment ago, a source of energy is needed to produce electrical generation. Now, pyramids are notoriously built on sites known to have subterranean water channels beneath them. In geology we call them 'aquifers'. These are basically interlinked rivers which are continuously flowing to the surface under the pressure of their source. This alone creates a small electrical current known as physio-electricity!"

"We're still keeping things simple here, right?" Hannah mocked as Halliday thoughtfully scratched at his goatee.

"Now, because of this, the granite chambers become flooded with electricity - which in turn is fed under pressure upwards to what has been described to us by the scholars, as the burial chamber, thus producing an electromagnetic field within the pyramid! With me?" he didn't look for a nod of approval and ploughed on regardless. "Good!" he chuckled. "Historians are right about some things, it's not all poppycock! They refer to the golden cap stone which at one point in time, sat atop the pyramid as a permanent fixture. Sadly, I can here hear them lambast me now! It was not solely for decoration purposes! And why would it be? Gold is an excellent conductor! It would have been used to transfer the negative ions created that were stored within the granite chamber via a golden superconductor and dispersed them into the ionosphere above – creating a wireless alternating electrical current! Thus," he paused for clarity "a power station!"

Hannah seemed more interested in the mechanics of the now disassembled lighter but questioned the revelation all the same.

"And you can prove this?" she looked up. "I'm sorry, obviously you can. Otherwise we wouldn't be in this mess, right?"

The Professor lost his radiance and didn't seem so animated. "Well, not yet."

"What the hell does that mean?" Hannah was taken aback.

"Not..." he was visibly deflated "yet."

Picking up the diary and waving it under his nose she exclaimed, "Professor, my best friend is dead! I'm presumed dead and someone's still clearly trying to kill the both of us! I'd say you had the proof!"

Halliday looked stunned.

"What is it?" she added, slapping the journal down.

"Perhaps?" he looked puzzled.

"Perhaps what, exactly?"

"Perhaps they think I *can* prove it!"

33

Officer Harrison awoke with a jump. The Intercontinental Expressway lurched to halt as the train's buffers engaged and recoiled, shunting the carriages against one another like a giant rusty accordion. He had been curled up foetal-like, his face pressed firmly into the rough fabric for most of the night, until he was violently nudged from his perch and banged his head.

"*Really?*" he exaggerated, wrinkling his poster boy features.

He rubbed his eyes, feeling his clammy forehead with his fingers, noting the rise in temperature and sat up. Loosening his neck tie he adjusted the cabin blinds and daylight came streaming into the tiny booth. Harrison turned away shielding his eyes from the sun as the silhouette of a broad-shouldered giant of a man eclipsed the window, outside the carriage.

Tweaking the blinds, he pulled out the cell phone from the evidence bag. The phone was still unlocked. No new messages. He scrolled down to the last number dialled: Spam, and his thumb hovered momentarily over the connect call button. Thinking better of it, Harrison minimised the cell phone screen and placed it back inside the transparent bag. Then, checking inside his jacket for his sidearm, he started to make his way towards the front of the train.

34

L.C. Halliday had spent most of the breaking dawn rooting through his leather bound diary. He recognised that the sands of time were not working in his favour, as he feverishly flitted from one page to the next. Regardless of what his pursuers may have believed, the Professor knew he had to find the so called 'smoking gun'. Without it, his career was undeniably over, or worse still, he would be killed. This only affirmed one thing. He had to be right. Surely he had to be, or he'd never have found himself back on the Intercontinental

Expressway and heading to the tropics, leaving behind a trail of sizeable destruction. It was almost six months since his last expedition. Head of a rather ragtag group of scholarly students, more hell-bent on topping up tan lines and nocturnal activities than anything else. He'd sat silently, both confirming and discarding plausible entry strategies for the giant stone pyramid from scribbled pencil notes and memory alike. He was certain this peculiar looking stepped edifice had some kind of message it was trying to convey. It was screaming at him, he was certain of it. But what was it? Where *was* this smoking gun? He had to find a way inside. Then, as if one of the giant limestone blocks of this puzzling pyramid had toppled from above, it struck him! There *was* a way in! It was obvious too and the Professor couldn't contain his joy.

"That's it!" he exclaimed triumphantly.

Hannah stirred with a jolt. "Huh, a coffee two sugars," she grinned.

Halliday was uncontainable with delight. "Of course!"

"What is it?" Hannah yawned.

The Professor ignored her and continued. "Why didn't I see it before?" he laughed. "Cenotes!"

"Would you like a tissue Professor?" Hannah giggled.

"Cenotes! Don't you see? They were never the sacrificial pools of crystalline azure taught on campus! At least they were never intended to be! It's the source!" he stabbed his finger down sharply on the tatty pages between them.

"The source of energy needed to enable the pyramid to function as it was intended! Just like the aquifers I was trying to explain to you last night! An external source of energy *has* to have a way in otherwise electricity cannot be generated."

Hannah rubbed her eyes, discarding the blonde hair piece and her, assumed, new identity with it. "I'm sure you know what you're taking about L.C., but does it really change anything? I mean, we're still on the run, right?"

Halliday straightened in his seat and glared at the young lady, slapping the diary shut. "I thank you for reminding me!" He cleaned the lenses of his rims on an exposed piece of chequered shirt tail and replaced them, tucking said shirt in and getting to his feet. "First things first!" he exclaimed, before adding. "Paulina!"

Hannah rolled her eyes and reached for a cigarette paper. Did everything this guy say have to be some kind of cryptic guessing game? "And Paulina is?" she snapped, irritated.

"A tour guide, you might say."

"Un-fucking-believable," muttered Hannah, under her breath and stole a glance out of the window at her foreign surroundings. It was the first time she had left the city limits, let alone the country.

This time it was the Professor who rolled his eyes, replying "I apologise my dear! My only presumption being that you did not know your way up river!"

"You've gotta be kidding me?" The colour in Hannah's face drained in almost an instant.

"Okay then. Paulina it is!" Halliday picked up the diary and began to make for the cabin door. Hannah wrenched his sleeve, almost pulling the Professor off of his feet and slumped below the window line, her face a picture of terror.

"Is it really necessary," he began, before Hannah muted his dissatisfaction with a firm hand clapped over his mouth.

"Ssshh!" Her eyes burned into him, her heart pounding in her chest.

A large shadow eclipsed the sunlight that had streamed through the break in the cabins blinds. Agent Neville patrolled the busy platform with two smaller looking official suits at his side and disappeared from sight.

Hannah shook the Professor as she spoke. "It's him! The spook! The one who shot us, me and Alex! Oh my God!" She let go and tried in vain to place them again out on the platform. Nothing!

"Slow down, what on earth are you talking about?" Halliday was visibly shaken by Hannah's violent outburst.

"Yes me and my, oh never mind! We've gotta get outta here!"

"No, no! Wait a moment did you say he shot you? This spook or whatever you call him - he thinks you're dead?"

"Yeah, I guess!" she said.

"You guess? Hannah this is important, don't you see?"

"What are talking about?" Hannah ditched her jacket after extracting her cigarettes and lighter, relacing her boots and frantically replacing her cap.

"The point being my dear, he's not looking for you, is he?" Halliday said with a hint of sarcasm. He thrust his diary into Hannah's hands but still struggled to let go.

"W-what are you doing?" she stuttered.

"I believe Sammy called it 'growing a pair!' They don't want *me* I'm certain of it! They want my notes, my diary! They won't off me just yet," he chuckled. "They'll want to know where *this* is! Now get to the river and find Paulina, she'll know where to go, trust me. Just show her my diary, she'll understand!"

Halliday released his grip on the journal with a shove and Hannah fell back into the booth as the Professor bolted out of the cabin door. Hannah winced as she hit the hard panelling of the booth and scrambled to her feet. She burst open the door to see the Professor waiting patiently at the end of the train carriage. The automatic doors slid aside with the sound of air pressure being released and Halliday looked back down the empty carriage toward her with a wry smile. Everything slowed. Professor Halliday shuddered with a jolt as twelve hundred volts of tasered electricity ripped through his body and he hit the carriage floor with a thud. His weak frame convulsed in spasm and his lips foamed as he went limp. Hannah gripped the door frame in a trance and watched helplessly as two shadow-like suits stepped aboard the train and propped up the unconscious lecturer between them. She was jolted back to the gravity of the situation as a large deformed hand clasped a large plastic handle and pulled himself inside the carriage. Tiny mirrored sunglasses turned to face her as he spoke quietly into a receiver on his jacket collar. Agent Neville stopped mid-sentence and lifted the tinted panels above a wrinkled brow. They made eye contact and held each others gaze for what Hannah felt like an eternity. Neville's cold emotionless face dropped and he momentarily looked as though he'd just seen a ghost. Perhaps he had. The agent dismissed his thoughts as the shaven headed apparition turned on her toes and crashed through the compartment door separating the carriages at the end of the aisle.

Neville turned to his two companions who unceremoniously scooped up a twitching Professor and, cradling him with military precision, exited the train. He coolly replaced his tinted lenses and with menace in his voice, announced "Get him to the helipad. This won't take long!"

35

Harrison wasn't, by his own admission, a 'morning person' and was furious with himself for thinking more about where his next coffee was coming from, than the initial reason he'd found himself groggily wading down the aisle of an Intercontinental Expressway carriage, somewhere in the middle of the sub-tropics. The connecting carriage door had bolted open and Harrison was shrugged aside with the full force of a leather bound journal crashing into his chest, and he fell to the side hitting his head once again, his pistol slipping from his shoulder holster and skidding silently out of sight. There was a stifled shriek and the clattering of hurried footsteps as Harrison picked himself up and was instantly alerted to the large white 'A' embossed blue baseball cap was left in the fleeing passengers wake.

Before Harrison could even draw breath to alert her of his presence, the carriage door almost left its sturdy hinges as it was kicked open once again from the other side. Harrison twisted his frame and kept low as a beast of a man went over the top of him and he pushed upwards from his hips, launching the pursuer off of his feet and crashing to the carriage floor. Agent Neville fumbled for the taser which now lay at his side from his tumble, but could only watch with agonising discomfort as Officer Harrison's boot came down on his crippled hand and kicked the taser from reach.

"No school today?" Harrison smiled, as he gazed down at his assailant and reached for a pistol that wasn't there.

The look of triumphant content disappeared in an instant and Neville registered it almost before it had happened. A smile of his own almost broke through the professional block of ice that offered it. Neville was back in the game. He kicked out violently crushing Harrison's testicles, winding him and sending him painfully to the ground. The taser was nowhere to be seen and Neville pulled himself up, launching a hard elbow into the side of Harrison's contorted face. He reached for his own holstered hand gun as a couple of giggling Intercontinental Expressway cleaners entered the carriage, and replaced it inside his jacket, concealing it from view.

"We'll finish this lesson another day, sonny!" Neville hissed and lurched onto the platform, the doors closing idly behind him.

36

Outside the carriage Hannah gulped for oxygen in the thick humid air and scolded herself for not quitting her addiction as she raced across the platform and out of what wasn't much of a station. It was a different world from the dreary metropolis she'd loved and left behind. There were no slick, suffocating, high-rise skyscrapers looming over her. No continuous drown of impatient cab drivers leaning on their horns and cursing. Nor the swarm of varied black and grey pinstriped suits, mutely commuting to boardroom business deals. The buildings were no more than two or three stories high, brightly painted like a rainbow of restaurants and hardware stores alike. The air was filled with new aromas and her senses were dazzled. It was vibrant. Colourful. Alive. Hannah too was alive and she intended to keep it that way.

There was a stir of angry voices in a heated exchange behind her and she kicked on without looking back, tightly clutching the Professor's diary. Her heart was racing and she could barely breathe. Hannah's eyes were bright with fear and she stumbled into the dusty street, spooking the grazing chickens into a feathered frenzy about her. The sun burned down in the early morning haze and haphazard draped awnings covered what appeared to be a market place up ahead. The bronzed looking locals were ant like, feverishly flitting from one spice stall to the next and joyfully haggling in their native tongue, all blissfully unaware of the cold-blooded assassin hot on Hannah's trail.

It was suffocating in the market place and there seemed to be no obvious way out. Hannah stole a wide-eyed glance behind her. The killer towered above everyone else and was struggling to wade through the tight spaces but he kept coming - as surely as the moon would arrive as it chased the sun.

Hannah gripped the journal even tighter, momentarily

wondering what was to become of the Professor. Dropping to her knees she scurried beneath the brightly coloured tabletops and nestled herself between the randomly strewn spice sacks at the feet of one of the vendors. She tucked her knees into her chest and reached for a discarded length of table cloth to pull over her head. At first the vendor appeared angry, presuming there was a thief toying amongst her aromatic livelihood, as she clutched Hannah's wrist with a less than impressed frown across a bitter brow. Hannah sat terrified, staring up at the haggard old merchant with a nervously twitching finger clasped over her lips unable to summon words with fright. The vendor tipped her head in thought and looked beyond her wares in the market place to see what had put so much fear into such an angelic face. Mirrored eyes reflected her own cautious smile as she gently released the grip of the pungent table cloth, precariously hiding the terrified girl from view.

37

Officer Harrison felt the side of his face and grimaced, shaking his head in self-pity. The cleaners in the carriage were arguing with each other but Harrison didn't understand. He checked for his sidearm once again, cursing at himself. He stooped down beneath the carriage booths and his head rocked with pain. He leaned under and inched his pistol closer with the tips of his fingers, grabbing the hilt. The weight of it was reassuring and he replaced it in his shoulder holster and made for the exit. The younger of the two cleaners was teasing his colleague, prodding and stabbing a dull looking object in his direction like some kind of tribal dance. The older gentleman was clearly not amused and he kept his distance barking undecipherable tones. Harrison cleared his throat, flashing his holstered pistol and badge, which had no jurisdiction outside city limits let alone three thousand miles from nowhere. Still, it worked. The cleaner shot a look of shock not dissimilar to the one the taser could distribute itself. He swiped the taser from him and stepped onto the dusty platform, leaving the cleaners to playfully continue their argument behind him. The agent and Hannah were nowhere to be seen. Neither was the Professor. Harrison ran his fingers through his hair and sighed with frustration. He placed the taser in his jacket which clung to him in the heat and heard it strike the hard plastic casing of Sammy's cell phone. Snatching it from the bag, he hit the connect button and waited as he scanned the area.

Hannah was in complete darkness. Her life was in the merchant's hands and she held her breath and prayed to a God she'd never believed in. The vendor had every intention of keeping her stowaway hidden from sight, but the sudden change in her heckled tone, fused with the over-elaborate animation only served to alert the highly trained senses of the assassin. Hannah's pocket started to vibrate gently and she swallowed hard in disbelief. Her cell phone chimed into life and her heart sank as she tugged at a rough sack at her side.

Neville forcefully ushered the merchant aside, ignoring her elevated expletives and flailing arms, whipping the musty cloth free, like a magician performing a trick at a dinner service.

Hannah exploded from the spice sacks ejecting a handful of crushed chilli seeds from the sack she was pawing at. A thick cloud of the deep red spice engulfed the agent and consumed his senses. His eyes were partially protected by his shades, but they still burned. The tiny The tiny flakes of crushed spice and seeds irritated his vision and he let out a thunderous roar of frustrated anguish, which served only to alert Officer Harrison on the fringes of the market place.

Harrison's ears piqued and he broke out in a cold sweat at the realisation the chase was still on. Firecrackers snapped and popped somewhere beyond the market awnings and Harrison upped his pace ignoring the dulled pain in his head.

It wasn't gunfire but Hannah wasn't certain. She wasn't hurt and she'd certainly not been shot. Not yet.

She plunged through a break in the shabby tent-like structure and what she saw was strange, shocking even! There were people everywhere. Zombie-like skeletons, dressed from head to toe in fantastical colour and decoration. Giant hollow-eyed skulls adorned the streets in fanciful attire while mariachi rhythms accompanied laugher and dance. It appeared to be some kind of carnival, a festival maybe. Hannah jumped as more firecrackers ripped up the dusty street and vibrant coloured beads were placed around her neck by smiling faces ushering her into the throng of painted faces. It was madness. But a beautiful madness, she thought to herself as an anonymous patron gently placed a flowery tattoo-esque skulled mask over her face and took her by the hand. Hannah didn't look back and cradled the diary as she was enveloped into a sea of dead men walking. Her heart and mind were racing.

Harrison entered the market and nimbly made for the far side where the locals had been stirred into a kind of frenzied panic. The large frame of his attacker squeezed irritably through the semi-laced awning and disappeared from view. Harrison checked and double-checked his pistol holster tapping its reassuring hilt. It was a comforting feeling after the train carriage incident but he swiped it from his thoughts trying to keep his focus. He pushed on through the aromatic walkways and finally peered through the gap in which the assassin had fled. Half expecting gunfire, Harrison instinctively crouched from sight, wiping his forehead free of the accumulating Harrison instinctively crouched from sight, wiping his forehead free of the accumulating sweat and jumped. "Fucking firecrackers!" Harrison blasphemed as they popped and crackled beside him. He checked the charge on the taser and got to his feet. He could see the agent was only a matter of metres away. He was shielding his lenses and systematically scanning the crowd. Then, he lifted his shades, as if for clarification, and squinted with satisfaction across the festivities. The bitch thought she'd got away, Neville smirked, spotting an awkward looking figure still feverishly clutching at the Professor's leather bound documentation.

Neville slipped his hand on to the hilt of his firearm and casually approached the unsuspecting victim from behind. Hannah stole a glance back and a sense of panic engulfed her once again, but this time she was rooted to the spot and found that despite the warmth and humidity, her hands were shaking uncontrollably. A forceful, bruising, jar in her ribcage weakened her at her knees, as Neville pushed the cold hard steel of his pistol's barrel firmly into her side.

"Tssssh! Easy Missy!" Neville hissed through clenched teeth as he leaned over her and gripped her shoulder with his free hand, which tightened like a vice. He pushed the guns barrel harder against her bony frame as she tried to twist free." Now, hand me the diary!" he insisted.

Hannah pushed the skull-like face mask over her cropped scalp and looked down at the Professor's journal with regret. There was nowhere to run. The game was up. She held the weathered binder out in front of her and winced as she looked away. She knew how this worked - she'd seen too many movies to believe this psychopath would leave her alive. She bit down on her lower lip and waited for the muffled gun shot that would surely end her life. It didn't come.

Instead, an oddly familiar voice chirped up from somewhere behind the assassin, but out of sight.

"You look *shocked*!" Harrison said with satisfaction and jarred the butt of the killers own taser hard into his spine as Hannah dropped to her knees. Neville was instantaneously stunned into shock and Hannah watched wide-eyed and cowered on the ground as the assassin's head snapped back in pain and his body pulsed as if possessed and collapsed, almost crushing her.

"Halliday, where is he?" pressed the handsome officer as he took Hannah by her hand and melted back into the crowd, as the assassin twitched and jerked unnaturally in their wake.

"He, um…how?" was all she could muster, shaking her head in disbelief. Hannah had no idea how the persistent officer had come to her aid and didn't want to think about the alternative scenario she was facing only moments before. She was still very much alive and it seemed she wasn't alone after all.

"Not now!" he shrugged. "The Professor, where is he?" he prompted, eyes drinking in his surroundings. Harrison's senses were on high alert as they pushed through the crowd. Everything looked surreal, a world away from the tired grey streets of the metropolis they'd left behind. His right eye had swollen, was bruising already and he winced as he mopped the sweat from his stinging face once again.

"They..." there was a pause, "took him! There was nothing I could do, I swear. He... he just!" her eyes salted, cradling tears and she offered the journal to Harrison, looking defeated.

He unclipped the leather clasp as they walked, trying not

to spill its contents onto the dusty street. There was a river system etched onto the open page with shorthand scribble which Harrison wasn't even going to try to attempt deciphering. Doctors were all the same, he smiled to himself.

"The river – that's it!" Hannah exclaimed stabbing a finger on the scruffy diary. "They took him up river – Paulina! Paulina knows where!"

"Paulina?"

"Yes, L.C. said that…"

"Elsie?" Harrison looked dumbfounded.

"Halliday, L.C.! He said to find Paulina! She'll take us up river!"

"Up river?"

"To the pyramid, I imagine! I'd guess we'd find him there too!" Hannah had found her spark once again and looked a little more animated.

"Slow down super cop!" Harrison laughed, but Hannah only took offence and tried to take the journal back, without success and scowled at him.

"I'm going with or without you – but I'll need that book!" she gestured to the diary Harrison was still slowly thumbing.

"Here, take it!" he said snapping it shut with a smile. "But you'll find it hard to take it up river!" He held the journal out like some kind of peace offering.

"And what makes you so sure?" she snatched it back and dusted it down.

Harrison stopped walking and exhaled impatiently. "There aren't any rivers on this peninsula!"

39

The rainforest was alive with the constant hum of unseen activity from within. Spectacularly coloured birds of various species sang and fluttered between breaks in the canopy high above, while howler monkeys called warnings to lofty perched neighbours hidden from view. A well-worn single track road wound its unforgiving path through the stifling humidity of the jungle and the old four by fours engine whined, coughing thick black smoke rings into the dust clouds its tread kicked up in its wake. Hannah sat blowing smoke rings of her own as she sucked the life out of the cigarette between her yellowing finger tips at the rear of the open-topped vehicle. Officer

Harrison was engrossed in the diary and waved away the smoke that was being blown rather annoyingly in his general direction. His head still ached, his shirt was wet through with sweat and his bare feet swung almost violently over the back end of the rusty old trucks tailgate. They'd been advised by the locals back in town to follow the ancient hunting path cut through the thick rainforest, marked out in the Professor's diary for the past handful hours when the toothless old driver whom they'd chartered the journey from, screeched the vehicle to a juddering halt and banged on the cabin glass for their attention.

Harrison sat back up, pulling his feet back inside and started to relace his shoes, as Hannah extinguished her cigarette on the pickup's hot metallic surface.

"What's up?" she said, tapping the glass with frustration.

The old man was making overly dramatic gestures with his arms and pointing into the thick foliage and waving his finger in front of his face.

"This is as far as he'll take us. It's the end of the line I'm afraid!" Harrison felt his bruised groin and hoped it wouldn't be much further into the dense brush.

"What d'ya mean, end of the line?"

"He says it's cursed." Harrison stretched and pointed

down beyond the tree line which seemed to diminish on an alarmingly steep decline to an open expanse of crystal-like water surrounded by high steep-banked walls. A naturally formed sinkhole, the *cenote* as they were known, had been created by centuries of erosion which had collapsed the limestone bedrock beneath, exposing the water that flowed silently underground.

The ravaged loincloth of a primitive looking scarecrow gently fluttered in the warm breeze above the hood of the old wreck, as the bony remnants of its twisted ribcage chimed a hollow song. Its empty cavernous eyes unforgiving.

Hannah was taken aback at what was staring back at her. Half man, half jaguar – complete freak out! She spat on the ground and tried to act like the warning of curses didn't bother her, although her stomach was making knots inside. The old boy took his fare and cranked the beaten four by four back to life. He was still flapping and gesturing as he slapped his floppy sun hat on the door panel and chugged slowly away in reverse gear.

"Cursed?" chuckled Hannah, silently recalling the past twenty four hours. "Spare a thought!"

Harrison giggled and looked back up at the scarecrow and frowned. It had kept the locals away and now *he* wasn't sure if he really wanted to know why. He checked his pistol and replaced it under his shoulder strap and looked at the diary for a bearing. Hannah was already picking a path to the basin's edge and appeared to be vying for somebody's attention. This girl will be the death of me, Harrison thought to himself breaking into a light jog behind her.

40

E.M.POWER had quietly purchased large portions of seemingly random and uninhabitable topography, forcibly flushing Paulina's people, natives, belonging to the rainforest for hundreds, possibly thousands, of years, from their homes, to see it destroyed in the process. Profit once again trumping heritage. Disease had culled the population and its cultures to the very edge of extinction and Paulina was one of very few who remained in the ever decreasing jungle habitat. She'd first met the Professor eighteen months previous on his first expedition to the 'new found' wonder of the world. Unlike most wealthy plunderers of her beloved heartland, the Professor was more acquainted with preservation than destruction and they hit it off almost immediately. She was the same age as the Professor but years of manual hardship in the unrelenting sun had stained her a deep bronze, her face more of an ancient treasure map than a stereotypical thirty something. The Professor had lost his parents at a young age too and this struck out a special kind of kinship between the two. The Professor promising that his research would one day make this economically ravaged land prosper for the right reasons again. "Give it back to the people," she'd recalled affectionately.

Paulina took an iron pot from the cooling embers and topped up a sculpted kiln-dried cup of warm honey and cradled it in her tiny hands. She contemplated her reflection in the cool water at her feet, wondering where her youth had gone and took a shallow sip, lost in her thoughts. Cave swallows dipped and dived by the dozen about her, feeding on the constant hum of unsuspecting insects that filled the cenote's cavernous bowl. It was a hypnotic melody which had been broken by the muddled wail of a stranger crunching through the brush toward her. Paulina sat up alerted to the unmistakable tones of a foreign tongue and wrapped her brightly coloured smoke stenched tunic closer to her body. Hannah bulldozed into the small clearing calling over her shoulder, as Paulina leapt to her feet clutching a small fishing knife – only the embers of the dwindling fire separating them. Officer Harrison stumbled clumsily into the fold, desperately tugging at the local flora that had happily attached itself to his sweat and coffee stained pants.

"Gimme a break!" he said, kicking the sticky vines free. Harrison almost knocked his companion into the hot coals and clung to her, more to stop himself falling than save Hannah from an all too embarrassing entrance.

"No gold here!" Paulina barked, her frightened eyes nervously probing. The knife she held was tantalisingly close to Hannah's chin.

Hannah stood muted by the rough looking blade yet transfixed by the strange woman's appearance. She was smaller in stature but had an overbearing presence about her. It was as if she was a small part of something much larger, part of the forest itself maybe. Her fringe sat just above her thin low brow and was chopped high above her shoulder, her leathery cheeks splashed with red ochre. Hannah wasn't sure if it was bone or handcrafted wood that hung low on her elongated lobes, but was certain whatever it was, had been expertly crafted by the serrated edge, which was now far too close to her face for comfort.

Harrison had seen his share of stand-offs and they rarely ended well. They were in the right place, they had to be, and he had to play this out right. If the information they'd been given was correct, there were no more tourism opportunities in the surrounding area. Since the find, the local community had been forced to source alternative means of income and cenote excursions were strictly off limits. E.M.POWER owned the land and forcibly penalised anyone who trespassed, putting all local money-making enterprises out of business, ensuring maximum privacy for the pyramid and its new owners. They were miles from nowhere, abandoned in the rainforest with a name as their only lead. Now though, their only chance of finding the Professor was warning them away and somewhat reluctantly threatening Hannah's life. Harrison slowly stepped aside and gently tossed the leather diary at the woman's jittery feet.

"Easy!" he said, showing his empty palms and backed away gesturing to Hannah. "Be cool!"

Hannah reached out for the officer's hand and gripped it tightly. Harrison nervously eased her away from the tip of the blade. "C..cool!" she swallowed hard and breathed in sharply, blowing out her cheeks.

Paulina's gaze was averted in an instant. The diary seemingly rendering her impromptu guests invisible! Dropping the knife, she snatched up the journal, then pushing them both aside, strained to see further into the brush from whence the strangers had arrived.

"L.C.?" Paulina stuttered excitedly. A broad white smile washed across her features and she darted about her camp fussing and tidying. "L.C.?" she laughed, caressing the diary and holding it aloft. She skipped into the beaten brush, returning a little bewildered. "L.C.? No?"

Hannah stood almost transfixed by the sheer beauty of the lush forest which effortlessly draped its often spiny twines into the dark cenote below. It was a beautiful abyss. "No Paulina! No L.C.!" She faced the tiny woman who dropped to her knees and began reciting some kind of incantation, as her eyes welled with tears, she reached for the sky, still clutching the diary.

Officer Harrison reached beyond the fireplace and grasped the cooled cup of honey and handed it to the odd looking woman. The same woman who had danced across the open fire and placed a cold blade to Hannah's face, was now huddled on the ground and seemingly inconsolable. There would be no second-guessing they'd found who they were looking for. "We need your help! Professor Halliday, he…" Harrison broke off as Paulina glanced up at him enquiringly, "L.C." he continued "L.C. needs your help!"

He took the diary from her and unclasped it to reveal a detailed hand drawn map of a river system now believed to be underground. Paulina understood immediately and picked up a small lump of chalk as she sipped at the clay drinking vessel. She wiped her eyes and pulled the diary a little closer and began to etch an image of her own onto the fragile journal. Hannah lit another cigarette and stared at the jagged looking symbol carved into the page. The image resembled a lightning bolt. An international symbol of danger!

"Yes," Hannah nodded "L.C. is in danger! He needs our help, *your* help!" Hannah pushed through the rough pages of the diary until she came to the image of the step pyramid, tapping it hurriedly as she spoke. "L.C.'s here Paulina, the pyramid!" The bronzed glaze faded from Paulina's face as her eyes lit up from inside.

"But he's in danger, he needs our help!" Hannah began. She pointed at the chalk scribble and continued, "The people who took him have been trying to kill us and they'll kill *him* too, I'm certain! Paulina, if you understand me," Hannah's eyes were pleading with the strange native lady as she spoke "we *need* to get to this pyramid before it's too late! These people will stop at nothing to find out what it is they think he knows, and the answer is possibly somewhere within this diary! The *py-ra-mid*, Paulina – do you *un-der-stand?*" Hannah exaggerated, sighing a little and looking to Harrison for support but it was Paulina who spoke next.

"I....can....help you, if....you....speak....faster!" she

giggled, "I'm a guide....not stupid!"

Harrison winced playfully, stifling his laughter as Hannah gently pushed him off balance to Paulina's obvious amusement. Hannah relaxed as she gathered up the diary and continued to recall the events of the past forty eight hours in extensive detail - shedding light over the grey areas Harrison had not yet fully grasped himself.

The mood in camp had lightened a little, but Harrison tried to contain his own racing mind.

As things stood, Harrison was certain he'd now crossed a particular threshold. In the eyes of the law he would be seen to be aiding and abetting a known fugitive and the ramifications would be disastrous. He hadn't reported in since the early hours of the previous morning, and his Captain, not the kind to pass up the chance to berate a subordinate officer, had not even crossed his mind – until now. The Captain had stated that it was an open and shut case. "Just a matter of dotting the I's and crossing the T's," as he'd put it, outside City Hall, and he'd not heard from him since! Captain Stacey was always the first person on his case, ranting and bellowing about being kept informed of his whereabouts and the particulars. Surely *he* wasn't part of some greater conspiracy? He wondered if he'd become a target himself. Harrison coolly eyed his telephone handset and pondered whether the case could get any stranger. Things certainly didn't add up, and it seemed there was only one path – or river to follow…

41

From the cenote edge it was a tranquil place of spiritual reflection, parakeets crowing to potential mates across the mirrored expanse below. Wild orchids blossomed on the steep walls, whilst creeping vines hung helplessly out of reach of the water they desperately vied for.

In reality, the world below was far more fearful and darker than Hannah had ever imagined. Bazaar, alien-like stalactite formations appeared to pierce the cave systems lofty shelter, like giant bony fingers being forcefully plunged through from above. The small droplets of water which lazily dripped from each skeletal digit were magnified and echoed as they hit the cold crystalline pool below. It was substantially cooler than beneath the humidity of the canopy and a chill went through her as Paulina clicked on a flashlight revealing the enormity of the black hole they had so willingly entered. All three sat afloat the crude vessel as it bobbed silently in the blackness. The small outboard motor was yanked into life and Paulina handed her crew a pair of musty smelling head lamps and took her place at the stern. It had been discussed, that since the Professor's last expedition Paulina had discovered a new undisclosed route in the river system, due to an irregular quake which hit the area within the previous week or so. Hannah recalled the Professor's talk of aquifers from the train and hoped his theorised entry point would prove fruitful, somehow helping the abducted lecturer wherever he may be. Now, it was up to the three of them to blaze a trail into the unknown.

42

It was almost midday and the jungle sun was at its zenith as the company's helicopter clung perilously close to the rainforest canopy. Cresting the horizon, it dipped into a winding valley of thick vegetation, the main rotor blade beating a hypnotic rhythm as it cut through the humidity. From above, the dense impenetrable brush was dotted with crystalline pools of blue that twinkled like sequins against the lush green tree line.

Professor Halliday groaned as he came around. The plastic cable ties cutting into his wrist, tightened as he jerked his hands upwards, failing to snuff the nagging itch that tickled the bridge of his nose where his spectacles had slipped. He was bound to the seat and nudged his wire specs into place with his shoulder at the second attempt and fidgeted into a slightly more comfortable position. The sound of the chopper was deafening inside the cabin and the Professor felt a pang of light-headedness as the craft banked steeply above the jungle. Levelling out, the horizon was a sight to behold. Halliday momentarily forgot the severity of his situation and was transfixed at the majesty of the stepped limestone edifice that rose skyward out of the suffocating wilderness. Strangely, it felt like he was coming home.

"Beautiful, isn't she Professor?" a somewhat familiar voice cracked through the static of his headphones.

The two shadow agents from the station were stiffly perched either side of him showing little or no interest.

"Your expedition reports were fascinating Professor. E.M.POWER offers their sincerest gratitude for all the work you've done!"

Halliday rocked back in his seat and pulled at his hand ties in desperation. The Fat Man shuffled to face him from the cockpit and smiled clenching his stale cigar between his teeth.

"Emmet….Montgomery?" sighed the groggy geologist.

"You look so surprised Professor!" poked the cackling oaf as he fidgeted in his seat.

"My work, I'd meant… I'd hoped to help usher the tyranny and greed of the corporate monsters into a new direction! Show the world there's another more economically viable solution to the impending energy crisis that's upon us! We've stumbled upon an ancient technology, the possibilities of which are boundless! We have the opportunity to supply the entire planet with a free, renewable, wireless source of electromagnetic energy - an abundant source with absolute zero impact on the surrounding environment!"

"Heal the world, Professor?" Emmet Montgomery grunted. "Why heal the world, when you can own it?"

Halliday fought to contain his tears as he pondered the impending gravity of his life's work and the ramifications for the so-called civilised world. This rediscovered age old technology, unwittingly placed in the wrong hands would only serve to enslave the planet once again by empowering the few. Humankind was standing on the threshold of a revolutionary turning point in civilised history and one man seemed to hold the key. Emmet Montgomery. The name wasn't lost on the Professor either. Halliday knew the origins of the name well. Montgomery was synonymous with 'the power of man', whilst Emmet, only a play on words themselves he had to admit – was far too close to 'emit', to 'release or give out'. The man had clearly lost his mind. Surely this power lusting psychopath didn't believe that he was doing the work his name bestowed upon him. Emmet Montgomery empowered with electromagnetic power. E.M.POWER.

The plastic cut a little deeper into Halliday's flesh as he twisted his unforgiving binds. "This is madness!"

"Some may say Professor, but isn't madness only a side step from genius?" he relit the cigar and turned to the front once more. "Your presentation almost cost us twenty years construction Professor. It may seem madness but I can assure you that the City Hall explosion was purely methodical."

"Methodical? It was delusional, you murderer!" he was beginning to weep again.

The rotor tail blade made a wide horizontal arc as the helicopter slowly descended below the canopy into a clearing at the foot of the pyramid. The choppers skids touched down as it was enveloped in a cloud of dust and the pilot killed the engine, pressing and flicking small handfuls of switches and gauges whilst the slowing blades whirred to a halt.

E.M.POWER had cordoned off the entire area and a high fenced perimeter had been set up encompassing the ancient structure. The entire site was unrecognizable from the Professor's last expedition. Flags snapped and fluttered as the company emblem, the lion at rest, proudly watched over its new domain.

"Oh Professor, you're a man of vision!" Emmet Montgomery unclasped his lap buckle and removed his headphones, exiting the helicopter with a thud. The two shadow agents cut Halliday's ties and unceremoniously wrenched him from the passenger cabin. "Surely, you can see the bigger picture? Did you honestly suppose the *university* had funded your globe-trotting expeditions across the four corners of the globe? I presumed you a smarter man than that Professor!"

"I presumed the world would benefit!" Halliday hung his head in despair.

"Ah, but it shall my good man!" Emmet Montgomery chuckled. "And so shall I!"

Halliday felt a sharp jolt in the base of his spine. Agent Neville appeared from somewhere out of sight and forced the barrel of his pistol into the Professor's aching body – a curt reminder that only *smarter* answers were going to keep him alive.

They walked around the nose of the chopper, the two shadow agents staying with the craft. Halliday needlessly crouched as he shuffled, not wanting to hit his head on the impotent looking rotor blade above. The heat was stifling and he slipped off his jacket after being cut free of his bounds and slung it over his forearm mopping his perspiring brow with it. Familiar sounds welcomed the Professor as he drank in his surroundings. He fantasised about his last expedition, half expecting Paulina to come scurrying from the brush, her face a picture of uncontained and refreshing excitement. But Paulina didn't even know he was here, nobody did…except maybe Hannah.

43

The cavern ceiling crept ever closer in the dim light and the feeling of claustrophobia intensified as unsteady flashlight revealed moist walls narrowing in around the crude vessel. There was less of an echo in the confined eeriness of this ancient water system, but every hundred metres or so the suffocating weight of the world above would momentarily disperse as huge dome-like amphitheaters would fill the black voids above them. In time, the weakened limestone would eventually erode away and collapse in on itself littering the lush jungle above with the crystalline sinkholes that were scattered across the jungle topography. At irregular intervals tiny trickling streams ran off the basin's edge, creating spectacular rainbow filled waterfalls as the sun cascaded in from high above.

Paulina clutched the rudder as the outboard motor gurgled lazily below the surface. Her face was bright with enthusiasm as she told exaggerated tales about her ancestors and the sacred spirits that were said to still frequent the shallows. This did nothing for butterflies that steadily built in the pit of Hannah's stomach, except maybe add a small handful more. Her eyes strained into the darkness and her heart leapt at the sound of a pair of boisterous parakeets disagreeing somewhere above the suffocating darkness. She grabbed nervously at the boats gunwale and looked to Officer Harrison for reassurance.

"Me too!" Harrison exhaled, appealing to the child-like side of the brave young lady who was clearly not at ease with this subterranean world. He relaxed a little and released the tension on the grip on his hand gun, which had dug a stippled crisscrossed pattern into his palm. Hannah smiled nervously back and almost plunged head first over the bow as their craft lurched to a halt without warning. The motor wheezed and spluttered so Paulina neutralised the straining engine, presumably cursing as she slapped the water and wailed into the dark chasm above.

Hannah regained her balance and straightened her headlamp, peering into the abyss as the boat rocked idly in the silence.

"What is it?" Harrison queried in Paulina's general direction, his tone hushed.

"The spirits!" she joked, poking Hannah with a bare callused foot and grinning jovially. Harrison grunted trying to stifle his amusement.

"Gimme a break!" she said, placing a damp cigarette in her mouth.

The tiller was jammed and it was clear the propeller and skeg had become entangled with the aquatic plant life somewhere below the boats keel.

Paulina took her knife from its sheath and tapped the steel motor at the stern which clunked and clanged back off of the surrounding walls. The only sound - that of trickling water which joined them from an ancient stream somewhere high above. Hannah lit the cigarette and exhaled, peering over the edge.

"Can't see a thing," she said, looking bemused.

"The flashlight, is it waterproof?" Harrison ventured to Paulina, beginning to unbutton his shirt.

There was little light but Hannah felt sure she was caught staring at Harrison's torso and she blushed in the darkness, looking away coyly. Harrison just smiled and continued to strip to the waist as the boat gently bobbed in its wake.

Paulina handed the rusty blade to the young man and moved away from the motor, crouching next to Hannah. "Sí, sí... but the water, it's cold and deep," she winked.

"That's….reassuring!" Harrison shivered, feeling the chill of the water as it seeped into his skin. He gently lowered himself in, gasping for lungfuls of air as his torso was slowly submerged into the lapping depths. Placing the knife between his teeth, he inhaled sharply through his nose and disappeared from sight clutching the flashlight.

"Be careful!" Hannah warned hesitantly. But he didn't hear her.

The water was clearer than Harrison had expected. The flashlight beam penetrated the wall of blackness, illuminating the microscopic world of the abyss beneath him. He kicked on, reaching out and grappling a slippery handful of aquatic vine, which had coiled itself around the rotor blade. He tugged at it vigorously and dropped the flashlight as he fumbled with the jagged edge of the knife. The feeble light diminished in a spiral below him and came to rest on the cenote floor. He cussed inwardly, yanking at the reed, his heart pounding in his chest. The entangled vine snapped free and the vessel shunted forward with the natural flow of the river. Harrison pushed for the surface and gulped for air as he resurfaced, splashing around in the darkness. Hannah's headlamp picked him out and Paulina whipped the motor into life, circling round to where Harrison bobbed in the azure.

Hannah flicked the remains of her cigarette into the void and grasped Harrison's forearm as the boat drew alongside him.

"The flashlight!" he panted, "I dropped it!" He pressed the blade back into Paulina's palm and went to draw a large breath. Hannah squeezed his forearm.

"Please…be careful!" she fussed. Harrison winked and slipped out of sight once more.

The cold bit into him deeper below the surface but the glow of the flashlight warmed him as he descended. Harrison silently fretted with himself for not bringing the knife this time. The river bed was thick with reeds and he fought with his own imagination as he contemplated the perils of becoming fatally entwined. He reached out and grasped the flashlights rubber grip, disturbing the silty bottom as something glinted off of the powerful beam in front of him.

Harrison's lungs burned for air and he kicked off the bottom, rising rapidly to the surface, almost thumping his head on the hull.

"There's something down there!" he gasped resurfacing, leaning his elbows over the wooden sides of the boat and panting.

"What d'ya mean, something?" Hannah bullied. Paulina was tending her knife, cheerfully.

"I dunno! The torch light it…..hold on!" He drew breath and sunk from view. On the river bed Harrison skitted the beam amongst the slippery flora and brushed at the dense black sludge it sprouted from. There! Something glinted back in the flashlight once again. He drew himself closer, reaching out, and tugged at the resting object as a child's skull materialised from the swirl of cloudy soup he'd disturbed. He almost drew breath at the shock as his heart leapt in his chest. The skull settled on its side and stared back vacantly at the, now unsettled, officer, as his hands fished around on the floor in front of him. The object he'd dislodged was short and conical looking, perhaps twice the length of the skull itself and it glittered in the flashlights dazzling beam. Tucking the flashlight into his pants, he scooped up both artefacts and pushed for the surface of the ancient cenote.

Back in the relative safety of the boat Harrison shivered as he replaced his shirt without a towel to dry himself first.

"What do you suppose it could be?" he queried, to no one in particular.

"Maybe the spirits?" Paulina offered. Although this time she wasn't laughing as she studied the tiny skull in her hands. "Maybe it is better not to disturb them!" She placed the skull on top of the lapping water and watched as it spiralled from sight and lay to rest on the river bed once more.

Hannah took the granite cone from Harrison, directing her tone towards Paulina who sat back next to the idling motor. "Less of the spooky stuff if you don't mind, it's not being rude I'd just rather not know... if that's cool with you?"

"Looks ancient," Harrison chipped in.

Hannah studied the relic beneath her headlamp and looked up in disbelief. She shook her head, rolling the engraved granite in her hands looking for some kind of explanation.

"What is it?" Harrison and Paulina spoke in unison.

"It can't be! Surely...?"

"Can't be what?" Harrison pressed.

"Erm...." She paused and giggled uncomfortably. "Ancient!"

"What do you mean? It has to be! It's probably rested on the riverbed for hundreds, if not thousands, of years, just like the skull!"

"As valid as your argument is... it's impossible!" She dropped the relic on the deck and wondered what the Professor had gotten her into.

Still shivering, Harrison picked up the discarded relic and pondered the ancient engravings.

"Certainly looks old to me! You care to enlighten us?"

"I can't be certain but...."

"But what? Certain of what, exactly?" The frustration was clearly straining Harrison's patience.

She took it from his grasp once again, looking it over for clarity.

"It's not an ancient text at all," she rolled it in her fingers. "This makes no sense!"

"What doesn't?"

"The text inscribed, it's a language alright! But it certainly isn't ancient!"

"How'd you mean?" Harrison looked intrigued.

"I think it's binary!"

44

At the foot of the pyramid, Emmet Montgomery stopped walking. He was wheezing and clearly struggling to breathe in the humidity as he gracefully dabbed at his forehead with a silk handkerchief. He turned to face Halliday and clipped the end off of a fresh cigar, chuckling delightfully, replacing the sweat-stained silk into his pocket. He probed the Professor through his monocle, subconsciously caressing the string of high quality pearls to which it was attached. "What has become of your diary, Professor?" he snorted.

"You spoke of construction….a build?" A firm reminder of Neville's presence enveloped him again as he felt the agents pistol press into his ribcage from behind. "I, I don't have it... it's..." he fiddled with a handful of hair, glancing up to the pyramid's summit. The barrel dug a little deeper and Halliday groaned in pain.

"This is not a game Professor, you understand!" Emmet Montgomery cracked his cane against the hard limestone surface of the pyramid behind him. He idly turned a grotesquely large leonine ring with his fleshy index finger and thumb, and lit the cigar. "A puzzle, it may be! But most certainly not a game! You see, I believe you have something of value which belongs to me. The final piece of this elaborate puzzle. Your research could never have been so conclusive had you not known about the particular artefact in question. Needless to say, had you complied with E.M.POWER in documenting and handing over all excavated artefacts, before deciding to make your own theatrical conclusions in the public domain, I sincerely believe your beloved Samantha would still be at your side today!"

Halliday recoiled like a snake waiting to strike and his eyes bore into the soulless oaf as he cowered in the obese man's shadow.

Neville warned again of his overbearing presence and violently shoved him off-balance.

"Ah, come Professor, a small sacrifice in the name of humanity, surely? Look around you! Sacrificial offerings were made on a daily basis by our jungle-dwelling ancestors in the name of the greater good!"

"Humanity? Greater good?" Halliday choked.

"Humanity, as you so eloquently put it in your City Hall rhetoric, needs an answer! A new source of energy for the masses! Energy which is not detrimental to the planet itself, as I am sure you are fully aware! Your humanitarian work is remarkable Professor, I really do commend you. I'm not an evil man…. just ambitious!"

The Professor flushed and fell to his knees. "I... I don't understand!" Tears welled in his eyes and he started to blubber uncontrollably at the foot of the pyramid, his life's work destroyed by a lust for power. E.M.POWER.

Emmet Montgomery snorted impatiently leaning on his walking cane as cigar smoke billowed in poisonous clouds around him. "Professor Halliday, it may come as somewhat of a surprise but you are not the first academically qualified geologist to have worked this particular site for the company. This marvelous structure was discovered over twenty years ago!" Halliday sat on the backs of his legs, staring through a mop of hair as the sun flashed off of his specs. His face was a picture of confusion as he swiped a sleeve over his salt encrusted cheeks. Emmet Montgomery wheezed for air, lowering himself to meet the Professor's child-like gaze and continued. "And thanks to the unauthorised lecture you conducted almost eighteen months ago, we had to go public about the discovery, before which the existence of the pyramid would have remained a mystery and you could have remained in the public eye. As it was Professor, well... I'm sure you're beginning to understand."

"Twenty years?" Halliday whispered, almost inaudibly, shaking his head.

Emmet Montgomery was grinning from one over-sized fleshy earlobe to the other. "Twenty years in the making, you might say." He stood again, marveling the huge megalithic limestone steps. "It is true, our ancestors were far more technologically advanced than the history books would give credit, Professor. Upon this fantastical discovery was a message, in part, but not as yet a complete one!" He motioned to Neville, who was holding a sturdy looking carbon fibre case and handed it to him. Chubby thumbs were carefully swiped across the fingerprint I.D. readers. There was a faint green glow accompanied by two successive beeps confirming recognition and the case locks clicked free accordingly. Emmet Montgomery set the case down on the base step of the pyramid, popped the lid and reached inside. He retrieved a conical looking piece of granite, approximately twelve inches long which glinted in the stifling sunshine and silently handed it to the Professor.

Halliday took the artefact, caressing it in his hands, noting the strange repetitive dots and slashes which adorned it, wide-eyed in speculation. The inscriptions were nothing like he'd ever seen. His hands were still shaking but no longer through fear. "A message, you said there was a…?"

Emmet Montgomery chuckled hollowly, snatched the relic from the Professor and shuffled a few feet from where he had been standing. "Antiquity has provided us with three of these wonderful relics. Messages, from the past! There is a fourth," he paused, "undiscovered relic!" the last part of the statement more of an accusation the Professor felt.

"I... I've never seen anything like it, the inscriptions, they... they make no sense! It's not a dialect I'm familiar with…" his voice was trampled by that of the Fat Man.

"Ones and zeros!" he boomed, his eyes were wild like a raging fire.

The base of the pyramid was littered with prehistoric scars and Emmet Montgomery checked his standpoint, examining the structure as his cane beared his weight. There was an apparent machine-cut scar, fresh and true, the same radius as the relic itself. Halliday felt a little embarrassed he had not picked up on the circular saw marks that jaded the smooth block work before, but said nothing, instead, wondering why these original parts of the structure had been cut away and concealed from him.

"Binary Professor, the mathematical language of the Universe! Our ancestors have encoded a powerful secret and entrusted it to us! They knew they couldn't sustain an entire global civilisation on finite fossil fuels, at the cost of the planets own natural harmonics! No! They never had too! They used the planets natural forces, forces that are all around us!" his arms were wide and expressive, a second and third chin wobbling in tandem on his fleshy face.

A thin smile brushed Halliday's dusty lips at the realisation of his own haphazard theories. "Wireless electromagnetic energy…" his jaw went slack.

"The codes were simple to decipher Professor, I'm sure most first or second year techies would have no trouble at all, hence the secrecy, you understand! Encrypted in the message are plans, a remarkable blueprint for a structure not unlike the one which it adorned." Emmet Montgomery was relishing the possibility of finally locating the missing piece to this megalithic puzzle and proudly mopped his brow. There was a minor disturbance in the distant jungle as howler monkeys haunted the lush canopy with echoing cries, witnessing a solitary jaguar gorging on its fateful prey. The Professor's eyes burned with fear and hopelessness at the thought of E.M.POWER dining at mankinds top table, whilst the rest of humanity helplessly thanked them for the scraps that were scattered before them.

"Twenty years ago, almost to the day, E.M.POWER began construction Professor! In an undisclosed location, far away from prying eyes, on the other side of the planet! Precisely aligned with the planets strongest intersecting electromagnetic fields and located in the geographical centre of the globes accumulated land mass, stands a structure of such magnificence and grandeur that it will presumably outlive time itself! Over two million, two hundred thousand, finely quarried limestone blocks, sit proudly beneath a golden capstone awaiting the final piece of the puzzle. The capacitor! An engine, if you will?" Halliday was struggling to take it all in, but Emmet Montgomery continued unabated. "But to start our revolutionary engine Professor Halliday, I will ask you to hand over the key!" There was a short pause. "The relic Professor, where is it?"

"You think I have a key?" Halliday said almost to himself rather mournfully. "I've never seen…"

Emmet Montgomery's face reddened as he clenched

down on his cigar. From Halliday's position it looked as though he would spontaneously combust at any moment, plumes of smoke billowing from his cigar, had engulfed his sweaty forehead. His cruel face twisted with dissatisfaction and he looked to Agent Neville and nodded abruptly. Neville brought a hard boot tread down on the back of the slumped Professor's knee and applied his weight. Halliday screamed.

45

The claustrophobia intensified as the subterranean river wound its twisting course into the eternal darkness of the cenote. They hadn't travelled far since their unforeseen drama with the rotor blade which had been quickly and bravely rectified by the now shivering rookie police officer. Harrison was feverishly rubbing his chilly biceps beneath a damp shirt and his teeth chattered uncontrollably as he spoke, causing Hannah to chuckle in the gloom.

"Think I get it n-now!" he clattered.

"Huh?" Hannah didn't look up. She was slowly turning the conical granite artefact in her tiny hands, squinting through the dim light of her headtorch and thumbing the peculiar engravings. Paulina sat silently, a firm arm on the rudder as the motor gurgled in the cold soup beneath the keel.

"It had me p-puzzled a little, f-for sure!" he was drying his locks with his discarded jacket as he spoke. "Your n-name on Sammy's c-cell phone....Spam, I get it!"

"Your point being?" her gaze hadn't shifted.

"You can read that stuff, can't you?"

"Huh?" her head snapped up, catching the quivering police man in the headlamp like a rabbit with nowhere to run.

"Binary? You can actually read it!"

Hannah adjusted the lamp, bobbing her head in uncertainty and pouting her bottom lip in unison. "Yeah, kinda! Should've stuck out the entire course but Alex didn't think...." she trailed off. "Nevermind!"

"Sorry I just thought that, Spam, well you know junk mail and all that, it makes a little more sense now," Harrison smiled.

"No, you're right it's okay. Just a little poignant that's all. Most people think it's cos I'm a techie geek, but Sammy used to call me it because of my taste in men."

"Huh? Maybe I don't follow?" Harrison creased his

forehead as he pondered the statement.

"Junk! Male!" she added with a wry smile. Harrison laughed out loud, feeling a warm glow inside him as Paulina killed the motor *and* the chance to reaffirm his offer of going for coffee sometime.

"This is it, we're here! Up, up!" Paulina was pointing to a naturally formed stairwell which climbed the depths of the cenote and wound down from a tight recess above them, thick with unforgiving natural flora. There was an eerie silence which consumed them all as they peered up at the intersecting rays of sunlight which pierced the broken canopy high above.

"I guess this is our stop then!" Harrison remarked semi-enthusiastically.

Paulina smiled a broad white smile which seemed to engulf the darkness of the entire cavern and shook her head. "No, no. Not yet!"

Hannah had the Professor's diary open on her lap, the relic resting atop. "Looks like it here Paulina, you sure?"

"Sí ,sí el terremoto, mira!" her face was animated and she was fumbling for the switch atop Hannah's headlamp, clicking it off and drastically reducing their vision in the gloom of the cenote.

"An *earthquake*?" Harrison motioned to Hannah as they bobbed between the pools of light which strained into the black void from above.

"Sí, el terremoto!" Paulina repeated, and continued to explain that there had been a sizable earthquake on the peninsula ten days prior which had cut off a number of the natural waterways on which they had been travelling. More importantly, however, it had revealed a new route which was yet to be discovered by E.M.POWER, or anybody else, for that matter.

Their small vessel bobbed in the eerie darkness and pitched to the side as Paulina hurdled the damp and splintering bamboo seating. She slid a small rusting tinderbox towards her with her feet and giggled happily as the boat rocked idly in its own wake.

Hannah switched her headlamp back on, her patience fraying a little. "If the pyramid is above us, what are we waiting for? We're wasting time guys, L.C.'s probably ….." she fell silent, and she was completely transfixed on the contents of the tinderbox as Paulina leaned across and extinguished her headlamp once again. Harrison's features were aglow as the fragile dent ridden box lid was unclasped and routinely flipped open revealing its mystical contents. At first Hannah shielded her eyes and looked away. It was as if the sun itself had been tucked away in this tiny tin cell and the cavern was illuminated almost immediately, exposing the newly formed limestone pathway which Paulina had been so animated about only moments before.

Harrison sat wide-eyed and mystified, unable to avert his entranced gaze.

"Los espiritas?" Paulina offered.

"Yeah sure, ghosts why not? Like my day couldn't get any stranger!" Harrison joked.

Inside the rusty box, Paulina had kept a number of emergency items such as spare batteries, band-aids and flashlight bulbs. Curiously though, the spare headlamp bulbs and LEDs were splendidly radiant as they twinkled independently, unaided by the batteries which lay at their side. Paulina took a small handful placing them in Harrison's, her smile almost as bright.

"He was right all along!" Hannah began. She held the Professor's journal opened out towards the others and resting on her knees, her delivery of speech quickened with excitement. "My God, he was right! The Professor was trying to explain it to me on the Expressway, something about a new form of wireless electricity! Electromagnetic something or other, I don't quite remember but it's all in here…..look!" Harrison was studying the tatty pages which had now been pushed under his nose. His mind raced as his gaze washed over Halliday's carbon crafted pencil etchings of pyramids and their internal architecture. Only now, it started to make more sense. Revelations of why the ancients focused on quarrying limestone monoliths with high magnesium deposits for the ease of electrical current distribution. The crystalline composition of the selected granite and its electrical conductivity and how this relationship is shared with the microchip technology in the age we live in today. There were scientific explanations for building such a purposeful edifice upon the aquifers, like the one which they now sat, and the process of physio-electricity, extracting the natural electromagnetic energy flowing from the source river needed for the structure to be enabled to discharge the negative ions into the ionosphere. The possibilities seemed boundless!

"Wireless electricity?" Harrison ventured mockingly, still disbelieving what he was witnessing.

"Free....wireless electricity!" Hannah added as she marveled the shimmering L.E.D.s. "No wonder someone's been trying to kill us!"

There was a painful twisted cry of agony from somewhere high above. Startled parakeets flapped clumsily from their lofty perch as the majestic tranquility was shattered beneath the canopy. They had slowly drifted from the water channel and into the open calm of another cenote. Pools of light cascaded into the leviathan from above and root vines draped over the sides, swaying in the gentle breeze.

Hannah craned her neck and steadied her headlamp, should it topple away from her and into the cold depths. "Prof.....!"

Harrison snuffled her cry with a large hand and a daggered look. "Ssshh..!" he hissed, through crazed eyes and gritted teeth that were now clearly under better control from the cold.

Hannah grimaced but said nothing.

"Vamos! Come, come!" Paulina was urging the young lady to follow her. She'd pulled herself ashore and clung to the slick rock like a lizard, her eyes darting accordingly as she slowly inched her way into the jagged limestone, quake-torn, passageway.

"But the Professor? L.C. he's...."

Harrison was routinely checking his sidearm and randomly aiming into the gloom and rechecking. He placed a warm hand on her shoulder and squeezed it softly. "I got this, its okay," he said, eyeing the naturally eroded stairwell which was overrun by menacing looking creeping vines. He placed the pistol back into his shoulder holster and winked at Hannah. "I'll buy us some time, go on…..go!" he ushered her towards Paulina who'd already begun to slip between the perilously sharp edges of fractured limestone and clutching free standing LEDs between her fingers and knuckles. The LEDs were radiant. Harrison plotted a path in his mind's eye, not relishing the prospect of the climb *or* finding what had caused the Professor's agonising cry from above.

Squinting into the void once again, he turned to offer some words of heroic encouragement but both girls were already gone. He watched almost mournfully as the diminishing reminder of the magical lamp light slowly faded from view. He pocketed his own dazzling LEDs and swallowed dryly, cursing under his breath as he began his ascent.

46

Beyond the damp slime coated interior walls of the haunting cenote, Hannah could feel the crushing weight of the Earth impose itself around her as she ventured deeper into the freshly torn limestone scar. The space was becoming increasingly tighter and she struggled to compose herself as a pang of fear bubbled in her stomach. Her shoulder blades grated on the rough edges of the dryer stone and her clothes continually snagged as she shuffled about the passage. Paulina was of a smaller frame but made the same slow progress, the tiny LEDs between her fingers dancing up and down the rock face and lighting the confined space.

Hannah was grimacing at the prospect of having to continue much further and to what cost, when she felt the walls were no longer inexplicably painful to push against. In fact, even the ground beneath her seemed to become polished, as a void in the rock opened out into some kind of subterranean chamber at her feet. The entire cavity was aglow as the LEDs twinkled in Paulina's hands radiating their surroundings. Hannah ran her hand across the smooth surface of the chamber, looking rather mystified. The chamber was made up of precision cut limestone monoliths from antiquity, yet strangely they resembled a highly polished marble with seamless craftsmanship from the modern era. It had a low imposing ceiling which was cold to the touch and barely wide enough for the pair of them to lie down. At about chest height there was a large stone missing, a perfect square and its sides approximately three feet in length. Hannah reached into the recess patting the cold stone, her fear replaced with nervousness and angst.

"I don't think it leads anywhere." Hannah's eyes strained as she probed the dark corners, shaking her head.

Paulina snorted a muffled chuckle and tossed the small handful of miniature bulbs into the cavity which scattered like fireflies, illuminating an ascending passageway which climbed further into the limestone masonry at a curious forty five degree angle.

"You gotta be shitting me?" Hannah regathered the tiny powerful beams and repeated the action. "How far does it go?"

A quick flick of the shoulders and Paulina giggled for real this time, "Inside maybe?"

Hannah had no idea of the scale of the enormous stepped pyramidal structure that reached for the clouds above them. They'd spent the entire morning underground travelling up river in a maze of darkness and she longed for lungfuls of fresh air, despite the humidity. If this was the way out she thought, then up it was. Her mind flashed to Harrison and the Professor and the millions of possibilities that could be unfolding somewhere above her. Searching for encouragement she ached for support from the handsome young officer she'd left behind. She shook the worry from her mind and removed her headlamp, entrusting her grip on the bundle of radiant LEDs she now clutched in front of her as she jiggled her body up and into the tight confines of the ascending passage. Their luminosity never dimmed but the suffocating passageway fought to keep her greater vision to a mere few feet. As she climbed, she kept one steady hand against the smooth walls noting there were no markings within the immense structure. She called down to Paulina, who was holding Hannah's headlamp at the bottom of the shaft maybe thirty feet or so below, and heard her voice echo above her. Paulina flashed the lamp in recognition below and Hannah craned her neck shuffling for position. There appeared to be a small cavity in the ceiling above her resting place. Holding her arm outstretched again she peered into the narrow void above. The sides of the shaft appeared to be damp and pointed directly to the sky but how far they went was impossible to tell. The well shaft it seemed was inaccessible and the only course to pursue was the steep passageway which led further into the unknown. She kicked on up the ascending angle, her heavy tread coping admirably on the finished surface. Another thirty feet inside, she came to the end of the shaft and patted the wall for confirmation. She anchored herself to look back down the passage but the ceiling had disappeared once again and she struggled to keep balance as she groped at the darkness. Bracing herself properly she gazed into another ascending passageway which mirrored the first and climbed higher still, zigzagging over the original passageway. Hannah sprung into the passageway and grappled not to fall back the way she came. Composing herself she tossed a single LED into the darkness beyond. The tiny bulb blazed a comets trail in the blackness and disappeared over an invisible ledge about twenty feet above her, out of sight but sill aglow. Her heart leapt and she slithered snake like towards where it had settled. Atop the shaft Hannah rested on her elbows on a shallow limestone plateau letting her feet hang into the rabbit hole void from which she climbed. The solitary LED shimmered in the tiny pools of water that had gathered at the edge of what appeared to be the top of the narrow inaccessible well shaft from below. Beyond the well shaft there was another passageway, this one horizontal and stretching into the darkness. Pulling herself up, again Hannah grasped for a ceiling that wasn't there but steadied herself quickly. Looking up, the ceiling space opened up into an imposing granite lined grand gallery. The megalithic pillars rose up on either side meeting somewhere high out of sight in the gloom above. The granites crystalline composition sparkled magnificently, just as they were highlighted in the Professor's diary. Hannah took aim and tossed another LED, this one into the horizontal passageway ahead. It seemed to strike a wall about twenty feet away but the bulb shattered on impact and there was nothing but blackness. She crawled around the well shaft, into the passageway and onto her feet as she checked her footing. Her arm outstretched, she followed her radiant palm into the tunnel but failed to see any further beyond the glow of the LEDs. The passageway ceased after another fifteen feet and opened into a larger empty room, the only redeeming feature being three more huge granite stones adorning the ceiling ten feet overhead. She studied the featureless room wishing she hadn't left the Professor's diary with Paulina and tiptoed back into the grand gallery. She smiled nervously to comfort herself and stared wide-eyed into the darkness despite the crushing weight of the ancient megalith that entombed her. Hannah blew out her cheeks and mopped her salty face with a clammy forearm and gazed above the middle distance. Surely not! The huge gallery was another passageway and her pulse quickened with the realisation. The giant shaft continued its path, again at forty five degrees and cut a path above the chamber she'd just been standing in. It was almost impossible to get any purchase on the highly polished surface and she scratched a slow and tiresome route upwards. After what seemed an eternity she paused for breath at the summit and waved her handful of fireflies into the darkness. What she saw, took that breath away.

47

Agent Harrison crept into the reassuring warmth of the jungle sun. His tired frame suspended almost thirty metres above the depths of the black cenote below him. He grappled with the slippery vines that cut into his skin and paused to compose himself as he finally left the eerie subterranean world behind. His hands felt sticky and sore and had become thick with congealed blood from the razor-like creeping vines that he clung to and he momentarily considered dropping the ancient relic that hindered his progression. Harrison gritted his teeth wiping the stinging sweat from his eyes and tightened his grip on the prehistoric granite artefact, realising he potentially held the Professor's life in his hands and pulled himself up the final few metres and free of the jungle sinkhole. Rolling onto his back, he gulped in the thick air as his heart leapt at the sound of a now familiar cry - Professor Halliday. Stumbling to his feet, he squinted into the treeline and froze in mesmeric awe at the stepped limestone pyramid that rose skyward from the lush rainforest about him.

"What the…?" Harrison's jaw went slack and his knees weakened at the prospect of another potential climb.

Again there was another agonising twisted cry of pain. Harrison broke from his daze, unclipping his sidearm from its shoulder holster and crouched in the thick unwelcoming brush. His hands stung and were shaking again as he checked the pistol magazine and chamber twice. He hoped Hannah was okay and struggled to put the endearing thoughts to the back of his mind, swearing in sudden surprise as a howler monkey barked somewhere overhead, making him jump and take aim at the canopy high above. Composing himself, he gathered his thoughts and studied the relic, the sun glinting off its conical sides as he tossed it in his hand and smiled, tapping the granite artefact with the barrel of his pistol. The inscriptions were baffling and he pondered Hannah's revelation at the possibility of it being binary and shook his head in disbelief. He kept low in the thick vegetation and crept slowly closer to the gurgled wails of Professor Halliday and winced at the pain in his own lacerated palms as sweat trickled onto the steel grip of his gun.

Before him, the tropical brush thinned into a sun scorched clearing at the base of the giant edifice, which seemed to be enveloped by high wire perimeter fencing, emblazoned with an all too familiar company logo. E.M.POWER. The lion watching over his domain.

A swollen red-faced man, whose features reminded Harrison of a cartoon swine from his childhood, looked peculiarly out of place against the backdrop. Standing with his hands clenched behind his back, his tailored suit a far cry from comfort given the hostile surroundings, the Fat Man looked to be enjoying dictating a well rehearsed speech as he admired the summit of the pyramid. Huddled foetus-like and pleading in pain, Professor Halliday shielded his eyes from the harsh sun *and* the butt of Agent Neville's firearm. Harrison silently pressed his stomach to the prickly flora, levelled his pistol crosshairs and craned his neck in order to best hear the conversation.

Emmet Montgomery turned to face the Professor and stooped proudly over the coiled geologist, his contorted features hugging the diamond encrusted monocle as he bellowed his sickening threats.

"*Nobody* is coming Professor. You *will* die today!" he hissed, leaning heavily on his cane. Neville leaned harder still on the Professor's knee joint and struck him viciously on the side of his head with the butt of his gun, sneering with pleasure.

"I've," Halliday grimaced in pain and spat a string of fresh blood from his mouth, "I've told you all I know! I'm just a lecturer, a geologist, there's nothing more, I swear it, my diary is worthless I assure you! The girl, she, she…!"

Neville stooped over the cowering geologist and raised his battered chin with the barrel of his gun, the Professor started to weep as he stared at his own beaten reflection in the agent's lifeless mirrored eyes. Neville grunted with satisfaction and leaned a little closer, his voice cold and barely a whisper. "I believe you Doc. I *really* do! And that bitch'll wish she was blown apart at City Hall with the others when I find her. And I *will* find her, I swear it!"

Officer Harrison broke out in a cold sweat and froze as a Pit Viper emerged from the loose foliage and silently brushed over his extended forearm and hesitated, momentarily meeting Harrison's terrified gaze before moving on again into the dense vegetation. Harrison wasn't surprised to find he was holding his breath and exhaled slowly as he watched it disappear from sight. Again he trained his ear to best hear the sickening one sided tirade at the foot of the pyramid.

"Then, this is the end Professor!" Emmet Montgomery announced ceremoniously. "Your untimely death will not go unreported, although not quite the world changing headlines I believe you craved, Professor Halliday. Terrorists are largely forgotten, you understand, and in time the relic will resurface and the build will continue. Don't be alarmed Professor, the world will certainly change. Only, humankind will bow to E.M.POWER and celebrate the patented technological advance in wireless energy that only *I* can supply!"

Officer Harrison's intense gaze fell away from the three men at the foot of the pyramid and to the blood stained granite artefact that lay by his side. He rolled it idly in the dirt and thought about what Hannah had said. The implausibility of the ancient text and its implications should the binary code fall into the hands of their pursuers. Harrison again fretted at the whereabouts and safety of the girl he'd left in the remote darkness of the subterranean labyrinth and shook it from his mind. It was the Professor's life that was at stake and only he could save it.

"Goodbye Professor!" Emmet Montgomery scoffed nonchalantly.

Harrison scrambled to his feet in the noisy brush, his firearm levelled coolly in front of him as he swiped up the relic with his free hand. He emerged from the jungle in the shade of one of the many E.M.POWER flags that loomed high overhead and roared at the battered lecturer's captors. "Freeze! Nobody move!"

The remaining LEDs Hannah held aloft danced off of the smooth finished walls of the highly polished granite chamber at the apex of the ancient structure, like the stars of unnamed constellations in the night sky. Millions of tiny crystals in the granites composition wonderfully illuminated the suffocating confines of the so-called 'King's Chamber'. In the centre of the room stood, what Hannah recalled had been described in history classes the world over, a flawlessly crafted granite sarcophagus. Rectangular in shape and sparkling as splendidly as the walls which confined it, Hannah marveled at its breath taking contents. It most certainly was not a tomb. She pulled herself clear of the slippery ascending passage of the Grand Gallery and steadied her footing as she stared in silent wonder. Protruding from the top of the granite sarcophagus were two horizontal wooden plinths, approximately three metres in length. Each plinth was resting within two golden rings, each ring adorning the respective corners of the golden mercy seat to which they were attached. Atop the heavy mercy seat sat two golden cherubim facing one another with their wings folded inwards and pointing to the other. There was barely any space between the winged cherubim only that of which appeared to be a tiny dazzling electrical charge, blue and vibrant as it snapped and crackled between its angelic creators. The Professor's words instantly came back to haunt her. "It is my surmise that the pyramid is a geometrically sound fully functioning power plant!" Hannah's face paled at the thought she was potentially standing in the very heart of an ancient power station as described by the nutty Professor and suddenly the brilliant LEDs made a little more sense as she studied them in her hands. Again she swallowed dryly, cold sweat breaking on her forehead.

"You've gotta be shitting me?" her lonely voice echoed solemnly off of the chamber walls. She held her fist aglow above the now descending passage from which she had emerged. The void seemed bottomless from above and she tossed a single luminescent bulb into the abyss and called after Paulina. The tiny light diminished from sight but there was no answer. She called out again in vain as an element of panic exploded inside her. Hannah staggered backwards on the cold hard stone and her heart leapt in her chest as she lost her footing. The megalithic granite slab she had stumbled onto seemed to give a little beneath her feet and slowly compressed into the floor itself, before crashing to a halt with a deafening thud. Then silence. Moments later another terrifying thud jolted Hannah into a panic and there began a harsh grating sound of stone upon stone and she struggled to keep her balance as the room about her started to radically change shape. The passageway had all but disappeared and there was no way out. She was trapped. The grinding of granite was deafening and loose crystalline dust rained from the ceiling as pure terror cascaded through her very soul.

49

Officer Harrison pulled his aching body into the clearing at the base of the pyramid, his gun still levelled on the agent from the Intercontinental Expressway. The giant man loomed over a sorry looking university Professor he was charged with bringing in the day before and subconsciously wished he had.

"Drop the gun, now!" He blasted his command towards Agent Neville as he closed the gap between them on the open ground. "Now, Goddammit!"

Neville eased his finger from the trigger and took a small step to the side as the Professor moaned inaudible groans of gratitude in Harrison's general direction.

"Officer, Hayden Harrison!" Emmet Montgomery looked animated, clapping his chubby hands in slow succession looking almost pleased to make the acquaintance. "Your father would be proud. I'm certain of it!"

The words hit Harrison hard as he tried to rationalise what he'd just heard. His father was dead, shot down in the line of duty some twenty years ago, but his reputation preceded him and wouldn't be hard to trace. One of the highest decorated men in the history of the force, Harrison certainly had large shoes to fill in his rookie year but the mind games were not going to work. Emmet Montgomery inhaled deeply on his cigar and turned to Neville with a twisted smile. The agent's oddly familiar features remained unchanged.

"Forget it Montgomery!" Harrison spat at the infamous energy magnate and shuffled his gun barrel between the pair, his nervousness visible as the firearm shook in his blood-soaked hands. "The games up!" he focused his gun firmly on the agent. "Drop the weapon….now!"

Neville was unmoved. He slowly raised his free hand and pushed his mirrored lenses clear of his eyes, fully revealing his weathered features. Harrison felt a pang of dizziness engulf him at an odd recognition in the older man's eyes.

"Hayden," the agent began. "Drop the gun…..son."

Harrison staggered back a few feet, the words echoing in his mind as he shook his head violently in despair, and dropped the relic on the dusty ground at his feet almost forgetting the severity of the situation.

Emmet Montgomery dropped to his knees and clambered

towards the discarded artefact at the officer's feet, and held it aloft wailing triumphantly as the ground started to slowly vibrate around them. At first, the vibrations went unnoticed and Harrison's world was falling apart at the unwanted revelation. Professor Halliday lay swollen faced in the dirt as he fiddled with his broken wire rimmed spectacles like a child afraid to inform an overprotective mother.

"It's a long story Hayden, your mother she…..another time maybe! I mean, why serve a flawed system when you can control it? Think about it son! This is the future, *our* future!" Neville looked to his superior for confirmation as the vibrations slowly grew in intensity.

"Earthquake!" Halliday exclaimed through a mouthful of blood, visibly shaken by his own unwanted observation. The buzz of the jungle had not subsided, but there were no signs of its inhabitants fleeing to safety amid the rumbling confusion. If it wasn't an earthquake, what was it?

A deafening grind of limestone on granite pierced their eardrums as settled dust and sand was shaken free of the stepped edifice from above and the entire structure began to vibrate violently and uncontrollably. The ancient sacrificial temple at the summit began to fracture and splinter at its sides and the smaller more manageable pieces to the stone temple began to vibrate free and topple dangerously downwards, crashing against the limestone steps and thudding to rest at the base. The four men scurried to the relative safety of the perimeter fence line and watched open-mouthed as the five hundred year old temple which had been erected at the summit to make inhuman offerings to the Gods, crumbled and fell away, leaving a sight to behold...

50

Hannah clenched her eyes closed tight, once again praying to a God she didn't believe in, and clutched the LEDs in desperation, almost crushing them in her tiny hands as the vibrating finally ceased. Shaking uncontrollably she felt the cool warmth of the sun on her neck as she finally opened her eyes again, the dust settling around her. The pressure plate she had stumbled upon had given no warning as it disappeared into the depths of the pyramid, setting off a chain reaction of ancient engineering which had pushed the hidden chamber to the very summit of the structure and into the open. The golden winged cherubim were fantastical in the light of day and Hannah squinted as she shielded her face from the harsh sun, it dazzling against the top of the solid gold superconductor encased in its hard granite casing. Gingerly, she got to her feet, releasing her hold on the remaining LEDs and stared across the lush canopy of the rainforest which sprawled an emerald ocean in every direction. Four ant-like figures crept slowly closer to the ancient monument, their stares transfixed at the transformation of the summit on which she stood.

Releasing her grip on them, the LEDs tumbled off of the harsh rock, tracing a path to the foot of the pyramid and coming to rest next to the Professor. Halliday was wide-eyed and his jaw slackened, his pain momentarily forgotten, as he reached out and grasped a luminescent bulb that all but confirmed his theorem. "And then there was light!" he smiled to himself. The granite artefact thumped onto the ground beside him, its mystique suddenly disregarded as the Professor watched Emmet Montgomery struggle with the megalithic stones he was so desperately trying to ascend.

A single gunshot rang out in the confusion and Harrison's legs buckled beneath him as he spun uncontrollably and lost his balance *and* the upper hand. The bullet struck him on the shoulder and he collapsed in the dirt as two black suited E.M.POWER agents entered the fray, guns levelled as they bellowed inaudible instruction.

Multiple bullets whistled past Harrison and he staggered

back on his haunches as he strained his neck muscles and glanced back towards the Professor and his father. There was another solitary gunshot, this time much closer. Neville's sidearm was smoking and the stench of sulphur filled the close humidity. Halliday was still marveling the tiny LEDs, blissfully unaware of the proceedings.

The closest agent crashed into the dirt as he was struck in the forehead by Neville's steady aim, the remaining agent skidded to a stop in a cloud of dust, obscuring his line of sight.

"Easy does it agent, hold your fire!" Neville ordered, spittle flying and gun at the ready.

Harrison was fumbling in the dirt for his handgun as he writhed with pain. "You too, kid!" Neville didn't look down and he didn't have to, hearing the scuffling officer sigh in submission and relax on the deck as he tended his wound. "Agent, lower your weapon and return to the bird. I want to be airborne in T minus Five! *That* is an order!" The suited assassin looked down at his companion, blood pooling from the bullet which had shattered his skull and understanding he was in his superior's crosshairs he lowered his weapon. "T minus Four, Agent!" Neville forcefully reaffirmed. The Agent disappeared along with the settling dust and Neville reached down for Harrison's discarded firearm, put it on safety and tucked it under his belt and cracked his neck. He replaced his mirrors and stared up to the summit of the pyramid. Emmet Montgomery's silhouette had blocked the sun from his peripheral vision looking like some kind of unnatural solar eclipse, his hands aloft as the bright blue arc of electricity snapped and crackled between the cherubim. Hannah was nowhere to be seen.

"Hannah?" Harrison yelled as he twisted in pain. "Hannah!" his emotions betrayed him as he started to weep.

"What's it gonna be, kid?" Neville looked down at his son and cocked his head, gun still levelled. "We can have it all!" The choppers main rotor blades whirred into life behind him, quickly picking up pace as they cut through the hot jungle air.

"I reckon he'll pass!" Hannah's voice pitched in through the din. Neville's gun barrel whipped around and the hammer was cocked upon instinct as he faced down the indifferent gaze of the young woman in front of him.

Hannah was unarmed, standing on one of the base stones of the pyramid and smoking the remains of a badly rolled cigarette. She spat onto the ground at Neville's feet and shrugged. "It's been a long fuckin' day, Four Fingers, and I'm guessing that you'll wanna see tomorrow? So, what's it gonna be?"

Neville looked down at his helpless son, then the insignificant Professor and motioned to the cold steel that was trained on the girl and sneered before breaking into an uneasy laugh. "Stupid fuckin'….."

"No….!" Harrison cried as Paulina emerged from the shadows and plunged her fishing knife into the assassin's torso from behind. Neville crashed to his knees firing off a succession of random shots into the air which echoed above the choppers menacing blades.

At the summit of the pyramid Emmet Montgomery rattled off his own misguided shots into the shadows below. Hannah leapt from her perch and kicked Neville's gun from his deformed hand and followed through with a harsh blow to the side of his head, knocking him unconscious and took the weapon in her own hands.

The Professor snapped up the granite relic and was helped to his feet by the ever-smiling river guide who kissed his cheek in recognition. Hannah struggled with the weight of the wounded police officer pulling him to his feet. Harrison winced as he turned from his father who was crumpled in the dirt while Emmet Montgomery wailed at them from above.

"To the chopper!" Harrison growled through clenched

teeth.

The remaining agent stepped off of the landing skid and Hannah watched the pilot wind up his preflight checks as the agent struggled with the dust that whipped up at his feet, blinding him.

"Drop it!" she yelled as her own weapon shook in her hand. The agent complied and hid his face from the dirty air and appeared to be blown towards the base of the pyramid and his superior.

Boarding the helicopter they instructed the pilot at gunpoint without any further confrontation and looked on as the aircraft climbed out of the clearing before banking hard over the summit of the pyramid and cutting a path back towards civilisation.

51

It was screened on every television channel the world over and would herald a new age in technology, as E.M.POWER would place the final piece of their puzzle within the greatest man made megastructure the world had ever seen. E.M.POWER, it seemed, had won hearts the world over. There would be no more extracting the life blood of the planet in order to create the energy needed to make this industrial merry-go-round function profitably once again. Wireless electromagnetic energy. E.M.POWER would now be heralded as saving the planet. At a price of course, nothing in this world is free from corporate tyranny. But as long as we survive, we'll happily pay.

Professor Halliday sat up in his hospital bed studying the cool granite artefact as the television screened a live satellite feed from the centre of the planets geographical landmass and the sight of the most fantastical megastructure known to humankind. Larger by far than the ancient stepped pyramid he had become so attached to, this new construction dwarfed the limestone edifice from which they'd fled. It stood on the world's largest natural magnetic crossroads and would be powerful enough to supply energy to the entire continent. Other similar builds were already under construction the world over and would be fully functional within a couple of decades. Halliday ran his fingers across the crystalline surface of the relic and looked up at the television screen as a now all too familiar Emmet Montgomery delivered his words of wisdom to the world. Behind him, a large military twin rotor helicopter hovered high above E.M.POWER's giant signature trademark, a magnificent limestone lion watched the horizon, its piercing gaze almost humbled by the sheer size of the majestic pyramid it presided over.

The choppers cargo swung idly beneath: a wonderfully crafted golden capstone. This, the Professor knew, was to discharge the negative ions into the ionosphere, which had been collected over time and stored within the golden superconductor within, thus enabling the entire structure to function as he'd theorised.

There was a gentle knock at the Professor's door which was almost snuffed out by the giggling which accompanied it. Hannah and Officer Harrison didn't wait for an invitation and slipped into the room hand in hand. Harrison's shoulder and hands were heavily bandaged and Hannah predictably stank of familiar stale cigarette smoke.

Halliday smiled irritably in greeting his visitors as he struggled to take in the events that were slowly unfolding on the tiny screen which was mounted to the wall behind them.

"*And...* Paulina?" he ventured, almost knowingly.

"Home!" they replied in unison, but it was the young officer who continued.

"E.M.POWER have handed the entire site back to the local community. Paulina's people, few as they may be, are returning to the land which is rightfully theirs, they've been granted immunity. What with the world's eyes on this fascinating new technological advancement," he was pointing towards the television. "Her people will surely prosper with tourism the way it is! They certainly won't be forgotten!"

Hannah smiled as she spoke. "She talked of seeing her family again before she left. *And* the possibility of starting her own one day....*Professor!*" she winked.

"Speaking of family?" the Professor pitched in as he winced at the stitch in the cheek he was tending.

Harrison stiffened.

"Your father, I believe, tried to kill me... on more than one occasion!" Halliday pressed.

"My father is dead!" Harrison stated abruptly, turning back to face the television. His face paled a little and he swallowed dryly.

The picture on the television screen crackled and distorted a little before refocusing again. The chopper banked away from the giant limestone lion, a solitary broad-shouldered figure clung vice-like to the open cargo doorway - Agent Neville.

An elated looking news reporter captioned in the corner of the screen, eagerly informed the world that the megastructure would beckon the dawn of a new technological age. Hailing an end to the ever encroaching nuclear arms race that had silently threatened to wipe out humanity as the world's superpowers squabbled between themselves. The youthful face of the spritely reporter continued her rhetoric, informing the world that the pyramid was not only geometrically sound but earthquake proof also – it would stand the test of time.

"Earthquake proof?" Halliday stiffened his back as he struggled to sit up in his bed. "Oh my God, we've got to stop them before it's too late…" his swollen face draining of all colour.

"What is it? You're scaring me! Stop it!" Hannah squeezed Harrison's hand making him wince and pull away.

"Yes! Stop it! We've got to stop it!" Halliday was energised almost instantaneously.

"What you talking about Doc?" Harrison looked unnerved.

"I'm not a… nevermind! The earthquake don't you see?"

"Here we go!" Hannah rolled her eyes in jest.

"The earthquake... in the jungle!"

"That wasn't a quake Professor, you *know* that!"

"No, there was a quake a few weeks before! Paulina explained to me about the passageway that led inside the pyramid!"

"So?" Hannah shrugged.

"So that's why you were able to survive inside! There was little or no electrical current being regulated by the capacitor, the superconductor!"

"Is he always like this?" Harrison joked.

"The earthquake must have disconnected the structure from the source which supplied it, the aquifer! It must have been rendered redundant therefore you were able to enter it unharmed!" Halliday looked terrified.

On screen, the chopper was seen lowering the golden capstone into place.

"Is this explanation available in a language that we can actually understand, Professor?" Hannah poked.

"The superconductor, it hasn't been dormant! It's been unregulated *and* charging. Put simply, it's been generating and storing unimaginable amounts of energy since the last global cataclysm which destroyed our undocumented ancestors who built it almost thirteen thousand years ago!"

"Meaning?"

"Meaning, they're about to potentially destroy the entire planet!"

"Is that even possible?" Hannah remarked nervously.

"An unregulated discharge of that magnitude would potentially be catastrophic! It could rip the planet apart!" Halliday slumped in the starchy white sheeting of his hospital bed and hung his head.

The television screen distorted and went blank and an odd reverberating hum began to fill the room. Harrison looked to Hannah and swallowed dryly as the hum grew in intensity accompanied by a steadily building vibration all around them. The pitcher of water that sat on the Professor's bedside table crashed to the floor, splintering and spilling its cool contents at Harrison's feet. The chrome finished curtain rings that moments ago hung idly above the drapes they supported began to chime uncontrollably on the rails to which they were loosely attached, as a state of panic could be heard from the wailing nurses who scurried about the corridors outside the Professor's room. The vibrations intensified as a continuous rumble of unnatural thunder ripped and rolled ever louder from all around them.

"It's too late!" the Professor cried, gripping the bed linen above the din.

Harrison pulled Hannah's tiny frame tight to his own, ignoring the pain in his arms and the terror which now encompassed them. "You think we got enough time for that coffee?" he joked in irony.

Hannah opened her eyes and stood on tiptoe, their noses almost touching and cradled the handsome officer's bandaged hands that were wrapped around her. "I doubt it!" she said before kissing his lips.

52

Once again humankind had become the architects of their own demise. Hope had again been trumped by greed. An ancient technological revelation which heralded to deliver a finite planet from its plundered resources, had corrupted man's twisted psyche and been sacrificed to elevate the enlightened few. A new era in free sustainable wireless energy had been compromised in the name of profit and destroyed the planet. One greed fuelled step for a corporate stronghold had triggered a giant stride backward for mankind. The devolution cycle continued.

Clouds of fury ravaged the globe for centuries and scorched the ancient lands of a bitter past. Violent earthquakes twisted the beauty of what had been and the oceans swallowed cultured civilisations whole. Supermassive glaciers moved across the planets topography, slowly grinding the memory of civilisation to dust.

In time, this violent constant would eventually succumb to the natural cycle of the planets processional clock, thus restoring a utopian sense of harmony once again within the natural world.

Those who had lived out their lives away from the civilised world, on higher plateaus and shunned society, had survived, yet a great number of those who remained eventually succumbed to famine and disease. Those who remained sought refuge in cave dwellings and returned to their hunter gatherer roots, the written word forgotten. Only survival mattered now. Far less than one percent of the global population had survived the cataclysm but, survive they did.

A stubborn breed is humankind and the end of days was a long time ago now.

Millennia have since passed.

Epilogue

The sun burned fiercely overhead and a light breeze swept over the hot sands, while Kiko watched them work. The finest stonemasons in the New Kingdom had been summoned from across the land, to fashion the majestic limestone edifice in the image of Ptolemy himself. He was a fierce, yet proud leader of the people and the lion-like features that would remain were a fitting tribute as his hard gaze watched over his domain. Kiko sat idly picking his nose beneath the shade of one of the many date palms that littered the giant causeway. He studied the slow transformation as more than a dozen linen draped masons on fragile wooden plinths steadily chipped away at the ancient limestone mane.

Kiko wondered if the masons enjoyed their work, picking up a smooth stone and crashing it against a larger rock he'd been resting his feet on. Clunk clang. Clunk clang. He beat them in time with the same rhythmic efficiency of the masters that toiled in the hot sun and winced as he struck his own thumb, crying out. He threw the stone in frustration, a decision he already regretted as his mother didn't hold back swatting the back of his head with an open hand from somewhere out of nowhere and he began to weep. His self-pity was short lived and his ears pricked at the sound of an ivory warning horn echoing across the plateau. The stonemasons dropped their copper chisels and stone hammers, frantically descending from their lofty apparatus. The hypnotic thud of copper on limestone was instantaneously replaced with the bellowing of orders from the pharaoh's men of arms. Bronzed soldiers with painted faces poured onto the causeway in their thousands, their muscular torso's shimmering in the sun. Generals foamed at the mouth as they barked instruction to lesser ranked members of the pharaoh's hoard. Mothers cried out for the safety of their children as they eagerly battened the wooden shutters which adorned their crude dwellings on the banks of the Nile.

Still the horn bellowed its long drawn warning. Kiko had never known such excitement. His heart quickened and he got to his feet half expecting to be dragged back inside by his mother. Thick clouds of dust and sand were whipped up around him as he watched open-mouthed, thousands of perfectly crafted flint tipped spears bobbing in unison as the pharaoh's men marched in colourful ranks to the edge of the city. His mother was nowhere to be seen and Kiko grasped the opportunity to steel himself a better look. The hot sand was kicked up behind him as he dashed into the throng of scurrying street merchants and soldiers alike. Large wooden trading carts creaked as they were tugged from their market place moorings by heavy snorting oxen as whips cracked about him. Kiko was wide-eyed in the mounting chaos and was almost trampled by a wailing commander on horseback that thundered down the causeway, joining the swollen ranks of the Pharaoh's army. His pulse quickened as another ivory war horn belted out its long drawn warning from somewhere out of sight, as he scurried along in the cool shadow of a giant limestone paw – Ptolemy's half crafted gaze above him pierced the horizon.

Kiko composed himself and drew a lungful of dusty air resting his hands on his dirty knees and craned his neck. The Great Pyramid rose out of the sand at his feet. He swallowed dryly. Over two million giant megalithic limestone blocks systematically cut and placed beside and on top of one another, had created a geometrically sound structure that had all the hallmarks of The Gods. It was beautiful. The function? Unknown. Although it would make a fine tomb one day!

A cold chill swept through him and he struggled to find the spittle for his callused hands as he began his climb. The unfinished golden capstone that crowned this limestone edifice glinted in the hot sun above him as he squinted towards the summit. The war horns blew. Kiko's heart pounded in his chest steeling a glance below. Lose sand and chipped rock was kicked free by his scurrying bare feet and disappeared as the rocks tumbled out of sight. He pushed on higher still, picking a rough path he'd seen the master masons take from the safety of the streets below as he'd tended his mother's chickens during the sun rise earlier that morning. Kiko stopped, terrified. He'd heard nothing like it in his short life. Clinging to a giant block like a camouflaged lizard he twisted his body, his exposed flesh scorched on the rough limestone as he pressed his back against it, wincing. He froze and his knees weakened. A booming fanfare of trumpets swept across the plateau from the horrifying horizon. Kiko held his breathe in anticipation, losing control of his bladder. A warm stream trickled down his inner thigh and pooled at his feet.

The sunlight dazzled against the shimmering ranks of the heavily armored legions that had assembled on the banks of the Nile. Crimson banners depicting a golden eagle snapped and fluttered in the wind. The trumpets ceased. From Kiko's lofty position perched high on the face of the Great Pyramid it fell almost silent, bar the wind that licked against his square cut fringe and tunic. He stood transfixed and terrified.

Short bursts of muffled trumpet rang out in unison with the clashing and clang of hard iron on well-worn chest plates and shields. The silhouette of a lone horseman broke from the marauding pack and galloped up and down the splendid ranks of men. His plumed helmet swayed in the breeze as he barked instruction and inspected his army. Finally he turned to face the city, reining the beautiful and muscular creature in with a powerful arm. More than three hundred thousand pairs of leather bound, ironclad, sandals, clattered in a rallying war cry from foreign tongues. The legions moved forward with terrifying menace. Slowly at first, then their pace quickened, with shields at the ready.

The lone horseman raised an arm in gesture to the men around him then dropped it, cutting the thick humidity in two. The midday sun darkened as a hundred thousand arrows sped skyward like a swarm of locusts arching above Ptolemy and his assembled men. Breaking into a gallop the plumed horseman brandished a short sword and bellowed a guttural cry of encouragement.

"For the glory of Rome!"

His men kicked on behind him, bloodthirsty and cruel. They screamed as one…….

"Hail Caesar!"

Also by RN Vooght

The Spirit in the Sky

'Ancient Cosmological Gods & Where In The World We Find Them'

Contact: Myth-illogical@hotmail.com

Twitter: @VooghtRichard

Printed in Poland
by Amazon Fulfillment
Poland Sp. z o.o., Wrocław